Mark Fitzpatrick is a teacher, writer, and scholar, specialising in the Weird and the Wonderful.

He has a PhD in Literature from the Université de Paris – Sorbonne Nouvelle, and is currently an invited lecturer in several Paris universities.

He is working on setting up a small alternative educational project, *The Hedge School.*

Originally from Cork, he spent twenty years in Paris, living in garrets and trying to get his novels published. When this proved to no avail, he began publishing his work online on his website *The Hollow Behind the Hearthstone. Unreal City* is his first published novel, but there are several others waiting in the wings.

He has recently moved to Aquitaine, where he lives in an eerie old house in a village full of mysteries and secrets, with his wife, his two children, a Wicked Uncle, and two and a half cats.

UNREAL CITY

First paperback edition 2023

THE
HIDDEN
LIBRARY

THE HIDDEN LIBRARY

LA BIBLIOTHÈQUE SECRÈTE

Book design by Irina Magdalena Tomici
Cover Painting by Justine Gasquet
Interior Illustrations by Molly McHenry

ISBN 978-2-494927-01-8

www.thehollowbehindthehearthstone.com

ACKNOWLEDGEMENTS

My heartfelt thanks go out to all the people who read, critiqued, encouraged, helped, and worked on *Unreal City* over all these years. In particular, I would like to say thank you to Loukia Banas, for your unending support; to Jason Stoneking, Chris Burke, Peter Ferenczi, and Mary de la Torre, my Paris writers; to Estelle Murail, Róisín Quinn-Lautrefin, Sonia Ouaras, Céline Prest, Marina Poisson, Shannon Delorme, Célia Galey, my Baker Street Irregulars; to Anthony Cordingley, Will Noonan, Tom Newman, James Creedon, my Gentlemen of Pleasure. All of you contributed to my writing, and my living, in those Paris years.

Further afield, invaluable critiques and advice were given by Kira Hagen, Jackie Dilworth, Melinda Reidinger, Sarah Falkner and many others. All of the denizens of the Hidden Library have been most supportive and strange, and for that I thank them.

Working on the production and publication of the novel with Colm Roche for the process, Irina Magdalena Tomici for design, and with Molly McHenry and Justine Gasquet for the sumptuous illustrations has been an absolute pleasure, and their hard work shows in the finished product.

As the novel grew out of, and fed on, my academic research, and indeed took me away from it at times, I must thank my research director Jean-Pierre Naugrette, who moonlights in the Unreal City himself. He, more than most, will understand.

My parents, Pat and Johanna, encouraged me since I was a little child to follow my dreams ... Little did any of us know what a winding path they would lead me on! I am blessed to have them, and their undying, unending love and support. My siblings, on the other hand, have sabotaged me at every turn ... Ciarán, Áine, and Maeve: I'm lucky to have you. Thank you for everything.

My wife, Laure, and my children Liam and Esmée have been a constant source of delight and nourishment, and have tried to be patient when I'm too occupied constructing Unrealities in my head to come back to Actual Reality.

Thank you, my Wicked Witch and my Little Witchlings.
I love you all in the world.

DEDICATION

This book is for my grandparents.

Sammy Fitzpatrick, Peggy Devlin,
Jim Clarke, and Margaret Mulholland.

From you, I inherited all my love of stories,
of tall tales and wild adventures, of sweeping
romance and family sagas. This book would not
be what it is without you, and neither would I.
You were the best storytellers and weavers of
words a child could hope to meet, and your wit
and wisdom will live on as long as I can write them
down, and others can come after and read them.

"So long lives this, and this gives life to thee."

EDITOR'S INTRODUCTION

Thomas Mulholland

The following text has recently come to the attention of scholars, after the identification of its author, "Florence de la Tour", as one of the several pseudonyms employed by the Scottish-Irish novelist and poet, Martin Caulder (1927-1992). Born in Edinburgh, Caulder lived a peripatetic existence, studying at Trinity College, Dublin, at the Sorbonne, and travelling widely. He fell in with Brendan Behan in Dublin, and featured in early editions of Anthony Cronin's memoir, *Dead as Doornails,* though removed from subsequent publications. Early success with his novels *The Exposition and Cavalcade* in the 1950s was followed by an abortive spell in Hollywood. His years in Paris, in the mid-sixties, were among his most prolific, and left us with his best-known books, *Absent Friends,* and *The Undecided.* While in Paris, he associated with the American Beats and French Existentialists, met his wife, Lily Bell, an Irish model and actress, and his future translator and collaborator, Antoine Mercier. Further unsettled vagabondage yielded ever-decreasing literary fruits, and, following the death of his wife in Paris, he settled in Cork in 1980. Back in Ireland he established himself as Writer-in-Residence at University College Cork. His final known work was *The Book of Lies* (Faber & Faber, 1981).

Unreal City was first published, as Mercier has now shown, by the Olympia Press in Paris in 1964, in its series of "Collector's Publications"[1]. Caulder entitled the book *The Devil in a Woman's Form,* a catchy name chosen

---

[1] Maurice Girodias's infamous d.b.s ("dirty books"), a last resort for many starving writers at the time, including Henry Miller and Alexander Trocchi.

more for its prurient suggestion of sex and Satanism than for any over-arching relevance to the plot.

For this new edition, we have reverted to the original title-page's *Unreal City*, with all its rich suggestiveness. Its publication has been made possible by the (slight) revival of interest in Caulder's work in the wake of M. Mercier's recent release of *Le vrai livre des mensonges* (Editions du Seuil, Paris 2008). Mercier's revised version of *The Book of Lies* is based on the original manuscript, left in the hands of Caulder's translator and confidant for almost thirty years. The manuscript purports to give us the original ending intended by Caulder, which sheds new light on certain autobiographical details.

The translator, however, has played his cards close to his chest as regards the actual English-language manuscript. We must reserve judgment on this "True" or "Real" *Book of Lies*, until scholars have had the opportunity to read past Mercier's translation, and into the "Real" *Vrai livre des mensonges*[2].

Thanks are due to M. Mercier for his help in procuring a copy of the long out-of-print *The Devil in a Woman's Form* (on the cover, a dashing young priest, in his anachronistic dog-collar and soutane, is depicted holding up a crude crucifix, while two women – one dark, one blonde – in varying stages of *déshabille* cower swooningly around his knees; the back of the book is filled with advertisements for various creams, unguents, enhancers, and philtres. No doubt Caulder would have laughed).

Unreal City itself is a strange, chimaerical beast; the purported author, Florence de la Tour, was a pseudonym employed by Caulder for his saucier hack-jobs, when he needed some of Girodias's welcome coin to pay his rent. Some of the other titles attributed to "her" (and billed as "translated from the French") will give an accurate picture: *The Maiden and the Murderer, Blood on the Chaise-Longue, Chastise me Firmly Monsignor!, The Ravisher Rides Again,* and so on. Most are without literary merit, and bear all the hallmarks of having been composed at

---

[2] Interested readers must be referred to the short biography of Caulder by Professor Cearbhal König, Ex-position: A Life in Letters of Martin Caulder (Cork University Press, 1994); the present introduction must, unfortunately, be brief.

white-hot speed, with only a porno-thesaurus and a children's textbook history of France to hand[3].

Unreal City, despite its inclusion in the De la Tour series, has fewer of the standard topoi of the sex/bondage/bloodshed Gothic formula adopted by Caulder for the others; the book is presented as being a republication, by De la Tour, of an original from 1920, a privately-printed text circulated only among the intimates of its author and compiler, a certain William Crowe, Esquire, of Crowe Hall, Co. Clare. Crowe's narrative introduces and frames a series of other documents, letters, diaries, logs of experiments, by himself, his associate, Stephen Devlin, and another participant in the events related therein, Thomas MacGilpatrick. These were to have taken place in Paris, in 1894. The reader will judge for himself the literary merit of the narratives that unfold.

However, there is one major point that does deserve to be raised: one must dismiss the idea that these are *true* primary-source documents, from the 1890s and the 1920s; the nature of some of the material is wildly unbelievable. On the other hand, it *is* possible that the texts were actually written at some time in the 1920s. The style, and the subject matter, is relatively untypical of Caulder. The speed with which he apparently delivered the manuscript to Girodias also points to this not having been (at least, entirely) his own work.

The problem with this reading of *Unreal City* is apparent even from the title: an obvious quotation from Eliot's *The Waste Land*[4], the dating of the manuscript as 1920 must therefore be seen as a literary joke, claiming precedence in the use of that title. Throughout the text, there are further echoes and intertextual anomalies which must have us date its writing to 1960 at the earliest. Certain lines and images in the text bear a close resemblance to what we know of Caulder's early poetic work[5]. The present edition attempts to draw

---

[3] As well as perhaps a certain quantity of psychotropic drugs: see the present author's "Caulder's Black Cauldron : Pornography and Peyote in the Pseudonymous Works of Martin Caulder", Journal of Literary Ephemera, Vol.4, No.3, Autumn/Winter 2008

[4] And therefore also an echo of Baudelaire, and Dante – see Eliot's own notes to his poem.

[5] The collection, Earth Works, an example of what he used to call his "sensual Celtic paganism", according to M. Mercier, is now lost; Mercier further tells us that he believes that this book may never have actually been published, only talked about by Caulder, with the object of "wooing women".

attention to such examples of these "clues" in footnotes as has been deemed appropriate by the publishers at Savage House.

Well aware that fiction is not the usual diet of their readers[6], I, your humble editor, wish to thank my publishers, my press agent, my copy editor, and my designer[7]. I would also like to take this opportunity to thank M. Antoine Mercier, whose very circumspect help and advice has been so invaluable, and so rare. It is to be hoped that M. Mercier will soon be up and about again after his recent accident, and that his sad convictions of persecution will soon be left behind.

We are also very grateful to Mrs. Angela Caulder, the writer's daughter, whose welcome at her home in Cork will not soon be forgotten. Her unfortunate inability to provide any clues as to the whereabouts of Caulder's last manuscript[8,] along with her incapacity to assist the efforts made for this edition in any other material manner may be put down to bad luck.

Thanks are indeed due to Professors Cearbhal König and Jack Brooks of University College Cork. Their advice, both bibliographical and personal, and their intimate knowledge of both Martin Caulder's texts and the man himself, during his period as UCC Writer-in-Residence, have provided much of the direction needed for the present work. Thanks must also go to my supervisor at the Université de Paris–Nouvelle Athènes, Monsieur le Professeur Jean-Pierre Maugritte, who had never heard of Caulder before taking me on as a student, and who now holds him in no very low esteem, equalled only by my own regard for the professor himself. I trust I make myself clear.

In the absence of a true scholarly edition of this highly challenging

---

[6] At least, fiction that bills itself as such, rather than "Hidden Secrets", and "Untold Revelations", or "Ancient Conspiracies".

[7] All of which burdens rest, unconventionally, though not uncomfortably, on the capacious shoulders of Walter Oates, at, and of, Savage House. If you're reading this, Mr Oates, I'm pleased and privileged to be working with you.

[8] The "Holy Grail" of Caulder scholars: whoever we may be.

and thought-provoking work[9], the reader will content himself with this modest effort, offered up in the spirit in which one must assume it was intended.

Thomas Mulholland, MA (PhD candidate)

Université de Paris–Nouvelle Athènes

December 2010

---

[9] Funds for which are, sadly, only too lacking.

UNREAL CITY

———

A novel by Martin Caulder

– writing as Florence de la Tour –

PART I

William Crowe's Introductory Letter

My dear fellow,

As requested, I enclose here the documents of which we spoke the last time you visited. You will find letters, parts of journals transcribed, some records of experiments, and some few little notes that I have seen fit to confect, to maintain the flow of the other various papers. I hope that this miscellany of fragments and memories, strung out on the thin silver chain of my reminiscences, will find safe harbour in your hands. Be gentle, for your eyes tread on my strangest dreams ...

All of the events recounted herein took place some twenty-five years ago; it was during the time of our studies in Paris, when Stephen Devlin[1] and I, having more money than sense, made a certain wager (as you know, of course, the parlous state of Devlin's finances meant that his lack of wealth was outstripped, at the time, only by his signal lack of sense). To this day, I feel a terrible guilt at the follies of my youth, and none more than this one ; Devlin and I were not the only ones concerned. If we had only known the turn that events would take, then I, at least, would perhaps have renounced the whole affair before it began. But it was Devlin who brought him to me, the young man soon-to-be-of-the-cloth. He had made a discovery, he told me, an affair in which we simply had to intervene. He swayed me easily, then, though he was ever the more impulsive of us two. Before long, he had sketched out his proposal to me as we nodded over our pipes in the drawing room of my apartments in the rue du Bac. It was early Autumn, I remember, of 1894, and the nights were already turning chill ; my man Scully had lit the fire for the first time that year, and we stood either side of

---

[1] Needless to say, both William Crowe and Stephen Devlin appear to be entirely fictional creations, though there was once a "Crowe Hall" in County Limerick, now in ruins.

PART I

it, a rather pleasant Madeira in hand, and talked of this and that, when suddenly Devlin convulsed with the recollection (he was always so dramatic in his bodily expression of sensation !), and shouted at me that he had a find, we must, we had to, take a hand in this young man's destiny. I was intrigued, and thus the dice were cast. Would that it had not been so !

You may remark that this sounds unlike me: perhaps. My philosophy, these days, has been one of quietism and withdrawal. When you saw me here at Crowe Hall last year, you observed how simply and soundly we live. I have chosen; my wife, my child, and a simple faith it took me many years to find are my bulwarks against the vicissitudes. Devlin, as I told you then, is now off pursuing God knows what dream of *"luxe, calme, et volupté"* in his strange desert oasis in Morocco. I miss his company. This new generation of young men, you'll forgive me for saying, seem to me to have heads so opulently *well-furnished*, but somehow so unutterably *uninhabited* ... It comes from an excess of education, and an utter lack of living, I might have once said. But the Great Tribulation that tore Europe apart these last years has enlightened. These new men are but half-men ; the ones who knew the banal horror of the salient have had their manhood ripped from them ; the others, shamed, unmanned, by their not going out for warriors, have had their *idea* of their own manhood docked. And now, of course, in our own land, the spectre of Civil War stalks far and wide. There is no man should now keep himself above the world, or outside the world, though it be a harsher, uglier place than ever. I myself might be accused ... But I served Ireland when called, and I will serve her again, though I am old, now, for a soldier.

To return to the question in hand (forgive my digressions ; they are burning out the landlords once more in my part of the world. We escaped it the last time. I pray we may do so again) ... As I say, young Thomas MacGilpatrick was the discovery of the day, and *le vin du mois* for Devlin. I thought it one of his whims at first, but when he described to me the youth he had sat across from at tea at the Comtesse de M_____'s salon ... Well, I let my pipe quite go out. Devlin himself became unduly animated, his pale, long cheeks flushed over their fringe of russet beard, his hair flaming up in its habitual wild tufts. In the light from the yew-logs in the grate, and the many thick candles burning high in their ornate sconces, he looked quite possessed, of an idea, of a vision, as he so often did.

The young man was of a singular beauty, he told me, and spoke in the gentlest accents of his native Cork, touched here and there with his mother's wilder Kerry inflections. He spoke of his studies, and his faith, of the faith of his people, both his father's Jesuitical learning, and his mother's simpler, yet how more ancient ! Celtic creed. He spoke with learned Latin tags, and was persuaded, at the piano (or the harp, I misremember ; though the Comtesse would have favoured chaunting to an harp) to lilt a melody in Gaelic, which he had from his mother. He and Devlin spoke of poets they loved, and of subtle questions of theology. The boy matched him on all, and discoursed most winningly on the Jansenists of Port-Royal. Devlin probed, and found that the boy had an almost shy passion for Shelley, and had read things in Blake and (whisper it !) Byron, which had troubled his vocation. His parents were upstanding folk though, and pleased to see their son a priest, and so he had been to the seminary, and was sent to the Continent, to Rome, and now to Paris, to the Irish College, [2] to expand his learning, and to weigh the weight of the crozier that he would one day, surely, bear. Devlin, by my fire, laughed, knocked out the dottle of his pipe, and declared that he'd see us both in Hell before he'd let such a prize be carried off for Mother Church. I fear he did not know to speak so true.

Aurevilly certainly had the right of it when he said that after certain books, nothing remained but to embrace the foot of the cross, or the barrel of a pistol. You know the choice that I have made ; the boy of whom it is here question, alas, took the other path. For you may be sure, Devlin cultivated him, and brought to his attention certain books : you know the books I mean. Yellow books, forbidden books, books bound in softest, strangest leather, inlaid with intricate, tarnished brass, illuminated with ink blood-red, and the midnight-blue of indigo, the purple of Belladonna. We have read those books, you and I, and we know the effect they may have on a young man, who has been cultivated, but sheltered, a hot-house flower that shrinks and withers at the touch of ancient frost, or blooms out anew, in stranger ramifications, in a climate it was never made for. Such was he, the man Thomas MacGilpatrick : a flower of the flock, who never should have strayed. Such were we, Devlin and I, poor shepherds,

---

[2] No record of any Jesuit Novice with the name Thomas MacGilpatrick studying at the seminary in May-nooth, or at the Irish College in Paris in the 1890s has been unearthed. That said, better-funded research might find an overlooked reference.

3

to so lead one away on whom God had His most Benevolent eye. Such was our wager : to divert this young Saint-in-waiting from his path, to tempt him, to harry him, to play the advocates of the Adversary. Devlin, we agreed, should have all the powers at his disposal, that the Earth has to offer. He was to be the World, the Flesh, and the Devil offering all with outstretched hand, its Kingdoms, its Riches, its Pleasures. I was to take the higher, but the not less dangerous road, and show to him the narrow ways and mysterious paths, to open his eyes to the Light from Beyond, to let him see that the subtle sciences held the greatest rewards. In short, we were to offer him mastery in this life, more than the Church could (which was saying much, for a denizen of our priest-ridden isle), more than medicine could, or common learning, more than the law ; more than the mere libertine, or gambler ; an intoxication more potent than the distillation of any simple fruit or flower. For the laws we proposed to have him trifle with were the higher, the darker, the more ancient ones. To Devlin's Dionysos, I would play an Apollonian counterpart ; the upshot was, we would have him, and the next world would be cheated of its spoils.

PART II

Devlin's Posthumous Letter from Morocco

Dear Crowe,

Pleased to receive your long letter, which I have attempted twice to read and let fall from limp fingers ... it will provide a welcome challenge to occupy that dangerous twilight time between the last dregs of the morning coffee and the first sip of a cocktail before lunch. There are days when it's all I can do to resist having Atem get the charcoal smoking on an enormous hookah at this point ; there are days when I do not resist.

The books you send – extremely thoughtfully, I'm sure – will be hawked by said Atem on his next trip into Biskra[1] (you remember him ? I had him over in London with me in 1913, the time we all got savagely trolleyed at your club and began blessing bread-rolls for people. He was prettier then, it's true, but the little guttersnipe has become terribly fond of me, and I fear that years of my spoiling has unfitted him for any honest lifestyle. I am loath to part with him, I must say). He'll buy some sherbet or hashish or some business to entertain himself with his ill-gotten pocket-money. Or a woman even, who am I to say ? It keeps him quiet, this tacit theft-and-blind-eye arrangement that we have. Besides, I salt it all out of the poor divil's wages, and he's none the wiser ! In any case, I would not have read them. What do I care for writers, or for the living now, in my posthumous condition ? It gives a man a desperately interesting perspective, being dead an' all.

I see that you, as chief executor (and sole mourner !) of my estate, are managing the servicing of the debts, and the upkeep of the women and children as best you can. Bless you my boy, what I ever would have done without your clear head, I ignore entirely ! You gave me a most rare and strange gift : to attend one's

---

[1] Biskra is actually in Algeria. See André Gide's *The Immoralist* (1902), and biographical accounts of his time there for possible sources for this section.

own funeral is wonderful enough (and such a eulogy you gave !), but to be sent reports on one's posterity while one languishes in Purgatorio ... Well, you are quite the Angel, my love, my laddie.

Ach, he's back, is Atem, and sulking and skulking. He loves to make resentful noise when he hasn't my full attention, as now. He was so terribly jealous of you always. I imagine he knows it's to you I write. I imagine he reads most of my mail too, incoming and out-heading. Or at least he would, if he could make head nor tail of my English. He still attempts to teach me the Arabic script from time to time, but I must admit, it remains Greek to me.

What I did read, yes, I see it here, you speak about the affair of that poor boy in Paris in, what was it ? 1897 or thereabouts, no ? I don't much understand this need you seem to have to examine, to pore over those long-gone days. Your current life as gentleman farmer, with your estates, your horses, your family ... is it so intolerable that you must return to those bad old days, probe them like a sore tooth, reach for them like the phantom pains in a long-amputated gangrenous limb ...? You torture yourself needlessly, dear lad. Take it from one who knows, from one who's passed beyond the veil: there is nothing. There is no judgement, no sin, no retribution. There is only this long long gentle slide into dissolution, the body's edges becoming vague, the mind's memories diffusing gradually in a dark substrate of dreams, visions, imaginings. I no longer converse with shining beings, or the ghosts of the dead, or the Dukes of Hell, for I see no apparitions in this calm, silent desert. No visitations. Only my mind, unmoored sometimes, seems to drift in Time. The past is never over ; it is endlessly passing, endlessly with me, present, simultaneous, near and far. The voices which once came with vile promises or ringing annunciation, now, they seem dusty whispers from the corners of my own mind, echoes of my past, and I cannot remember who who was, is, becomes. My own mother's face ... I see more clearly the greenish face and dark-gold eyes of a nymph who stared at me from below the surface of the black river in the town where I lived as a child. I reached for her, I fell in. They said I would have drowned. She was the most beautiful, terrifying, melancholy thing. Perhaps all that happened after was the search for her, all my seeking, all the experiments and quests. I did not just want to touch her, child that I was, though her pale limbs, furred with flowing weed-tendrils ... I wanted to save her. To take her hand, and help her break through that glassing surface that imprisoned –

Forgive me William, forgive me. Forgive my scrawl, my ramblings. No, there is no forgiveness, no need. I remember, I said that. No forgiveness, no expiation. No matter how you plumb those depths, you will never find the bottom, never get to the bottom of the Abyss. It never ends. And so you will not, I fear, find what you are looking for. I leave those last sheets there, which may or may

PART II

not be legible ... I broke off, to sweat and tremble, and weep, if we are to believe Atem, the foul-breathed little liar. He put me to bed, he says, finding me fallen on the flagstones in the roof-garden, away from the shade of the parasol he had installed above my table, staring at the sun, shaking, crying. He tells me these things, I think, to convince me I am ill, and that I need him, and his medicines, and his ridiculous little prayer-scrolls sewn into my clothes. I tear them out ; he sews them back in : another game we play. I shouted at him earlier, when I found myself in bed, and my letter smoothed out, dried out, the stains barely visible, as you see. Whatever they are. I told him I cannot be ill, for I am already dead. He muttered some sort of folk-charm against evil. I am sure he feeds me poison in my coffee, and laces my sweet tobacco with far fouler intoxicants than the ones I ask him for. My policy towards food is simple : I eat none now, for I am beyond the need for such base sustenance. I know he doesn't wish to kill me. That would be easy, and he is also deathly afraid that I will haunt him, terrorise him, and be a disease in his family and his descendants to the seventh generation, as I have often promised him. He knows what I am capable of. Was capable of. No, he only wishes to keep me dependent on his kind ministrations.

No food, no, but the soul must eat, from time to time ... I will ask Atem for a feast tonight. He will bring some of his many younger "brothers" and "sisters" to this place. The girls are delicious little things, fleet as gazelles, gluttonous as jackals, the boys dark angels, golden-skinned, eyes like midnight. They are of some depraved clan like the Ouled Naïl, [2] who consider prostitution and lewd dancing a holy calling. They will be fêted, feasted, drink their fill, smoke and incense will mingle, and the drums and wailing pipes will turn wild. I will descend among them, and they will writhe around me, tearing, scourging, fondling, devouring. I will pass like a phantom, for they will not see me, they will only feel the flush of my hungry eyes drive blood beneath their skin, and their frenzy will mount, their ecstasy. I will watch them, from my couch, and choose, perhaps, one or two, and point them out, and Atem will take them off to be prepared ...

But I should leave off these reveries. You never had the taste I do for flesh

---

[2] I must protest, Mr Oates. I thought that this footnote was of true scholarly value. You say anyone who cares can look it up. If that's the case, then what's the point of my editing of this text at all? Since you will not reply to my emails, perhaps I can get your attention here.

and blood. I'm surprised you managed to father any spawn at all on that pale plump little heifer they married you to. You always disapproved. You never knew the pleasures, the pain, or that they are the same. Now that I may consume nothing, consummate nothing but flowing, fluid things, liquids, vapours, smokes ... You might imagine that this floating world of mine, in my palace in the desert, is my punishment. Tantalus in his pool. But no, there is no justice, no damnation. And I have created an oasis here, and the little children come unto me, they do. In the central courtyard, there is a reflecting pool, and sometimes, under the surface, among the black feathery-finned fish, there is something, I think, something, and a mournful golden eye seems for a moment to stare back unblinking forever –

I close. Atem comes with a pipe prepared for me. He will lead me to my couch beside the Western balcony, for the sunset bends the desert air most interesting, most purple. I give you all the papers you ask for, I give you leave to do as you will with them. You saved me, after all, so many times. And this last time, you ferried me across, away from the painful shore, with all its wants and wounds, and miserable tiny weights of the everyday, and into nothingness, into the vast silence of the sands, into my own, private, personal ever-afterlife. You deserve to have your way with all the stories I can tell. After all, you do me the great favour of organising far more tedious affairs than these, for those I left behind, in the lurch, or otherwise. I hope that one day you will find what you are looking for, in sifting this mummy-dust and these putrescent remnants of our youth. I hope you may one day make your peace, for I fear you will never be able to do as I have, and simply let go. I have found it, that peace that passeth understanding. It is called

[Devlin's last letter to me ended thus, with no signature, no date, and the papers out of sequence, folded haphazardly in an envelope on which an approximation of my address had been laboriously copied out, more drawn than written. I have not heard from him since. It would not surprise me, nonetheless, to find him on my doorstep tomorrow, hale and hearty, ready for adventure. – W. Crowe]

PART II

PART III

Thomas MacGilpatrick's Letter Home

Paris, Collège des Irlandais,

22nd Oct. 1894

Dearest Milly,

    Hope all is well, little one, and that Mother and Father are not driving you too hard for the exams. Don't worry! You'll be shot of them before you know it, and never have to become an old grey man before your time, like myself, bowed endlessly over my books, and burning the candle at both ends, and in between! But let me say again: listen to Papa when he says you might get a place at the University[1]. Lord knows, few enough are the young women who have not only the ability, but the opportunity... "Many are called; few are chosen ..." Not even so many called as all that, you might say. Ah, I can hear your dear voice, telling me of your school-room triumphs and trials... and telling me off for not writing since my last, in September. But you have no idea the things I've seen since then! I thought to save them up for you, so's to present you with a nice long letter, and to reassure you that I have not forgotten your Exams, nor again a more (and most!) important date that is coming up before too long...You'll have your parcel, as every year. No matter how far I go, I'll send you news, and gifts, and hope to make you feel reassured that I'm still out there, seeing the great world

---

1 Queen's College Cork admitted female students from the 1880s, and the first women in Ireland graduated in Medicine there in 1898, over 20 years before Oxford allowed women to take medical exams. The first female professor in the British Isles, Mary Ryan, was appointed to the Chair of Romance Languages in 1910. [I see. So historical footnotes are fine, as long as they're about feminism? I hope the typesetter (ie, you) remembers to delete these comments]

(and not only its libraries, I promise), and telling it "wait", for a brighter star than me is on the way... Milly, you'll see these things, I promise. If I have to come home and kidnap you, and tie up Papa and Mama in a cupboard under the stairs!

They're well, I hope? I would write again, but Papa never answered me, the last time. You'd think they never sent me to the schools, and to college, the way they spoke this Summer. It was a sore time, I know, for all of us. And I know that you blame me, but their idea of what I was to do, to become, was not mine. I know that Mama dreamed of my returning to Nanna's village, and them lighting the fires down the road to greet me, of all the old folks blessing me, and her, and all the young mothers bringing their babies for me to lay my hand on their heads. But she has a wrong idea of what path I'm on now. It is not to be a Parish Priest in South Kerry, I know that much. What it may be, one day... But I will leave off these maunderings.

No, I must tell you: that I have found within me this strange thing they call a "Vocation" is as much to my surprise as anyone's. But it is not only to serve (though I will do that) God, and serve His flock, but it is also to learn, to study, to think. Perhaps to teach, and perhaps to go further, to discover, to embark on a great Quest, for within this Church, and within our Faith, there are Mysteries, my dear, such as you can hardly imagine; it is not one thing, continuous, flawless. There are places, in this Church, and on this Earth, that are dark, that are secret, that are lost from the Light. We must have the shepherds, and the pastoral duties that they fulfill, but surely, even now, in this late day, there are still Crusades, and the Holy Mission of bearing God's Light in darkness, and giving battle to His Adversary, wherever he may be found? But I'll stop this. You are tired of your old brother and his sanctimonious blather, no doubt. Will you forgive me, if I'll tell you some strange and wonderful stories of Paris? I know you will, *a chroí*, [2] and I know you'll tell me stranger and wonderfuller ones, from the wilds of the end of the garden, at home, or the strange lands you roam and invent in that peculiar head of yours, away in your attic with your books...

Strange and wonderful... where to start? I mentioned, in my letter in Sept., the odd enigma of Brother Pierre, at the Irish College; he remains a

---

2 Irish : Darling (*lit.* 'my heart')

mystery, and becomes, if anything, more mysterious by the day. Did I mention the smell? Oh, Milly, it is unworthy of me I know, but the man reeks! Positively pungent, MacGillycuddy has nothing on him... He still greets me with his strange mix of English, French, Latin, and Lord knows what other languages he may be mangling in his mutterings. One of the other students here, a certain Damien O'Hanlon from Wicklow, tells me that Pierre has been here longer than anyone can remember. He swears that the old monk, if that's what he is, is actually *Irish*, and that he spoke to him once in the Irish language (though *níl aon Gaeilge ag Damien*, [3] of course ...). I think Damien is only going along with a story repeated to him playfully by some of the older *collègiens*, who are having some fun at his credulous expense.

Brother Pierre maintains his stony watch on the gates of the College, night and day it seems. He begins to shut the great doors on the first stroke of nine in the clock tower, and the keys turn, the bolt shoots home, exactly on the last toll of the bell. I once scampered past him as the clock began to mark the hour. He gave me such a look! Shouted after me: "Have no doubt, *jeune maître Thomas* (as he calls me), the *porte* will shut whether ye are *rentré* or left in the outer Darkness, with those that wail *et se grincent les dents*!"[4] It fair put the wind up me, I can tell you. He carries his bunch of keys with him everywhere, heavy keys, great and small, iron and silver and brass, clanking and clinking through the halls. Damien says he's heard the keys ring and rattle in the upper corridors at every hour of the night. They say, Damien informs me, in a whisper over breakfast, that Brother Pierre's keys are even heard above, in the great library, after it's shut at night, and below, in the corridors beneath our feet, where there's I-don't-know-what... (by the by, breakfast is miserable porridge still... I must suggest to D. that we slip out, pretexting early Mass in Saint-Etienne-du-Mont, and break our fast on fresh pastries and coffee at a counter on the Rue Mouffetard, with *le vrai Paris*).

And O, the sights Milly! The glorious Luxembourg Gardens with their turning leaves! The little children sailing boats on the great round pool... I have sat an hour together with those children, watching the Guignol puppet shows

---

3 Irish : Damien has no Irish.
4 Matthew 13: 37, 41-42. [well, alright then. No more Bible-references, unless dealing with Apocrypha, Kabbalah, Numerology, or the Suppression of The Evidence for Jesus' Marriage to Mary Magdalene. They're your audience, Mr Oates]

PART III

under the plane trees. Guignol's a kinder sort than Pulcinella or Mr Punch though, and it feels less off to cheer for him than it does to shout for a murderous, lying, wife-battering, baby-killing Punch...

But I forget, have you even ever seen a Punch and Judy? I know I saw one in Dublin once, when I was at Maynooth in the seminary. But I'll bring you the next time, I promise. Though you are perhaps too old now for things like those. Wait until you are but a little older, Milly, and you shall go looking for those childish things you once put away so ruthlessly. Do not be too quick to shuffle off those immortal toys, and games, and stories! You'll tell me I preach; I do, but you must listen. I am only twenty-three, yet already I long for the Lost Demesne of which you are still Lady! There are things that we only understand when we are children, before we lose sight of that Ever-undiscovered Country over the hill. You are not yet too grown up, I'd wager, to get an eerie thrill from Mr Punch's shrill cackles, or to have the Hangman and the Devil haunt you for nights on end, after you've seen them dance across that little street-stall stage ...

Do I seem over-sentimental, Milly? Do I make you out an innocent, as if your hair still fell in ringlets, and you lisped and played with dolls? I know, you'll be telling me – or not telling me, more like – of sweethearts next, and suitors, and then, who knows, of a wedding, one day? I am not sure I want this for you. The thought may be far from you, but there is also the Life of the Mind, upon which, as I have said, you have the choice to embark. They say it's difficult, for a Woman, to renounce all hope of living truly as a Woman, a Wife, a Mother, if she is to take the "unnatural" step of being further educated. I say it's not so clear. After all, look at me! Have I not renounced much, sacrificed much? I would hate to think though, that one day our parents might not see their grandchildren, that for many golden days, your life, and mine, might not be made bright by a younger generation, to still remind us of the undiscovered countries that forever remain to us, in childhood.

Do you think of these things, ever, Milly? I must admit, I do. If I have not mentioned them before, it's perhaps because it is so much easier to do, when far away, and when we each might be spared the other's blushes. And perhaps, re-reading your last letter, you seem to me now to be such a fine young woman, so wise and so sweet, so much a friend and confidante to me as well as a dear sister. But pay no heed, if this talk makes you uncomfortable. Write back to me of exams, and lighter chatter, and I shall get the message. Or do not write, maintain a chilly silence: and I shall hear it loud and clear.

PART III

Onwards, onwards! Other things. I take up the pen again, subsequent to a mildly disgusting dinner, which, if nothing else, has cured me of my melancholic reveries. The soup was swimming with some unidentified – though surely rancid – oily substance; the bread was stale, the meat cooked grey. And yet I hadn't noticed, truly; had, if anything, been rather comforted by the food in the refectory, so much does it remind me of the fare we used to have to tackle in the Halls at the seminary. But I have had my eyes opened Milly! I have tasted such food! I must tell you how it happened, for all else has been preamble. You must hear of my meeting with two utterly fabulous personages, as well as a Countess! Imagine her not being the fabulous one! No, the Countess, though very kind, and awfully grand, was *not* the interesting one; was not supposed to be, I fear, for she only hosted the *salon*. The interesting people, one assumes, were the ones invited, and for that reason. And how did I find myself at the Countess's salon, I hear you ask? All quite simple, dear, and all a most amusing misunderstanding.

I was walking down the Left Bank, towards the Jardin des Plantes, one sunny afternoon. My eyes had become red and itchy from the dust, the small print, the drudgery. The Bibliothèque Sainte Geneviève, fabulous place though it is, had become to me a "sterile promontory", [5] and all the while the sunlight streamed down through the vast high windows! I was compelled to leave, and my feet sought the river bank, and headed downhill, and east, through the markets at Place Maubert, and down the Boulevard Saint-Germain. Strolling then, heart light, head high, eyes bright and on the horizons, their roofs, spires, smokestacks, their long, lazy barges porting coal down the glimmering river, I was accosted... No, I was Hailed, perhaps, by a *most* unusual gentleman.

He was sitting on the wall beside the footpath, and letting the sun strike his face, a drawing pad on his lap. As I got closer, I noticed two strange things: *primo*, his eyes were *not* closed. They were wide open, and staring at the sun ; *secundo*, his hand, nevertheless, moved fluidly over his drawing pad, and seemed to be producing, rather than any kind of sketch, some strange patterns, surrounded by signs and sigils (I perhaps fill in a little detail here that I only perceived later, when he showed me his pad of drawings and notes and diagrams...For yes, you

---

5 The readers don't care about the patterns of Shakespearean imagery, you say? Fair enough. I'll consider myself warned.

will deduce, we came to be on terms of intimacy, in a way). But wait! apart from his queer attitudes, what did this man resemble, I hear you interject. I shall tell you, in these words: A Fox. Nothing, so much as a Fox.

His flaming red hair is slightly long, but stands up and out from his head in waves and tufts, especially when he has been thinking, and running a hand through it. He has close-cut gingery whiskers about his chin and cheeks, and his moustache is rather magnificent, bushy, waxed at the tips, and foxy red. It gives him the air of having something of a smirking snout, just like a fox. His hat was set beside him on the wall, a brown bowler, which he snatched up and flipped onto the side of his head at an angle that could not be more rakish, when he jumped from his perch to grab my arm. He wore a rather loud checked jacket, in a sort of green and purple plaid, which he has assured me since is the height of style, as well as garish trousers, gaiters, and shoes that look surprisingly down-at-heel for a man so obviously interested in playing the Dandy. On closer inspection, his clothes are much-patched, much-brushed, much-mended, and slightly too large, though obviously well-tailored. I wondered to myself: is this a man fallen on such lean times, that even his clothes hang loose around him? Or is this a man so *used* to lean times, that he scrounges clothes off his betters (and his largers, apparently?).

A mystery. An utter mystery. And so here he jumps, ahead of me, with a little hop-step off his wall, gathering his pad under one arm, wielding his hat with the other, sweeping it round his flamboyant bow, donning it again to shake my hand...

"Young Master Thomas, I believe?" was his opening gambit. I stopped in my tracks, utterly befuddled. "You must come with me! I believe we have an appointment with a prestigious gathering of our elders and betters!"

And with that, he whisked me off. A cab was flagged, and we were in it, an address was given, all before I had time to catch my breath. My improbable kidnapper turned to me, and offered his hand once more to shake.

17   PART III

"Please allow me to introduce myself, " he said[6]. His accent was Northern Irish, beyond a doubt, but much softened by years away. "My name is Stephen Devlin, and I don't believe we've met."

What strange fun we had that day! How different seems Paris to me since we met! Devlin is a terrible rogue, but so humorous, and so clever, that one must forgive him some foibles. An artist, as you'll gather, and a *most* interesting man. That day he brought me to a grand *salon* in the home of a Countess of his acquaintance – the one I've mentioned – a beautifully-dressed, wonderfully cultured lady, who greeted Devlin as an errant nephew, and chided him for his neglect. He presented me to her, and to the company, a gathering of pale, frowning literary men, languid ladies, and frighteningly polite aristocrats, their speech near-strangled, so mannered was their pronunciation. It soon became apparent that he had quite mistaken me for another Thomas, a portly boy of fifteen who arrived with his Maman, and was fed sweet-meats by that long-suffering lady all afternoon, pouting at having been upstaged by his namesake. The ladies were all quite fascinated to learn that I would one day be a *curé*, and had no end of questions for me. Many were of quite dubious theology, such as that from young Mademoiselle des Hermies, who asked if it were true that a certain Princesse de Y_____ had gained the secret of Eternal Youth from the Devil in the form of a giant black cat, and must now visit Hell once a month to pay the interest of her debt, in the form of... Well, I shall pass over the form of her payment; it shocked me that this young lady, younger than you perhaps, could unblushingly put words on such an idea, and in polite company!

Devlin drew me away from the crowds, and quizzed me on subjects philosophical, philological, mythological, archaeological, literary, scientific, and theological. His own thoughts on these matters bespeak the best kind of self-educated mind; here is a man who has filleted great libraries, with no guide but his own nose, and a sort of questing, burning light in his soul that leads him to the heart of things! He promised to bring me to his studio, to show me his canvases, and to show me the Paris that he sees, a carnival of strangeness and beauty. Doubtless, many of his beliefs are quite unorthodox, but it was so

---

6 No Mr Oates, absolutely not. 'Sympathy for the Devil' was released in 1968, so that doesn't help my argument. Please stop adding your own footnotes, and let me do my job. I am well aware that Martin Caulder met Mick Jagger in the late '60s, but again, this is 'evidence' of nothing.

refreshing to hear his great awe and wonder in the face of the world.

He tells me, for example, that there are Presences abroad in all Nature, and that these are not, as some maintain, malevolent fallen angels, but only the Forgetful People, whose processions, dances, and battles can be seen by any simple, passionate soul. This was charming, in the manner of the tales of the Fair Folk we used to hear from Mama. But when he spoke of Magh Slécht, the Plain of Prostrations in the South of Ulster, and of the unspeakable rites that were observed there, of the Seventh Plague that struck down the king Tighearnmháis[7] as he worshiped, with thousands of his men... It made me shudder, and I bade him change his talk.

He is not a rich man, though of good family. They are fallen on hard times, and he has struggled with his decision to pursue his dream of Art, rather than follow his father into architecture, or to study Law, or another profession which would enable him to help them. His inspiration is such though, and his animation when he speaks of Poetry and Painting! One cannot help but wish him luck with the pursuit of such a vocation. He told me that he would show me to see life as a carnival of sights and wonders. When he heard I sang, as I let slip through inadvertence, he pressed me into giving them a verse or two. The room fell silent! He drew me to stand before the hearth, and clapped and announced my song in some overblown manner. My cheeks were flaming, I can tell you, and the only song I could think of was an old one Mama used to croon to us, perhaps you remember? It's called *Siúil a Rúin*, you know, the one that begins: "I wish I was on yonder hill, 'Tis there I'd sit and cry my fill, And every tear would turn a mill, Is go dté tú mo mhúirnín slán"... She used to sing many songs, but when you were only very young. I wonder, do you still know those songs she sang.

But such a strange thing happened! My voice wavered and cracked, but I'm sure the French only took it for emotion, and were obviously much impressed that I would sing entirely in a strange, half-dead Celtic tongue (I think they never noticed that the verses are in English!), but I felt awfully self-conscious in among

---

7 Irish : possibly translated as 'Lord of Death'.

PART III

all these fine people with a song coming out of me that smells of oul' turf-fires and frieze coats, and "biled spuds for the supper". And then suddenly, from nowhere, there was a swell of music, tingling, twinkling chimes that swept around my voice and held it up, weaving in and out of it, dancing under and along my tune, and embroidering fine filigrees to it. I sang up stronger, and looked around, and over by the window saw Devlin standing, above a woman sitting at some strange type of box-harp, the strings stretched out before her, and her hands running over it; in one, two little silver hammers played, and glinting hooks and plucks were on the rings of the fingers of the other. I couldn't see her clearly, for though Devlin was in the curtain's shadow, she had the evening light falling in behind her, and I only knew her hair shone silvery and her dress was dark.

On the last chorus of my song, the rippling notes faded to a trickle, lightly falling through the air, and then two voices came and surged and blended with my own, one man's tenor, shadowing mine in close harmony, and a woman's... singing some strange counter-melody, drawing us all down with her to the end, to a whisper, and the last lights of the plucked harp-strings winked out. There was a long silence, and I saw the Countess hide her face, for there were tears on her cheek.

Shaken, I felt beside me for a couch, and sat, and there was a slight stir, and then a buzz of talk, and people coming and going, speaking to me, thanking me, praising me, asking me questions. I could say nothing in reply, for my mind was all aflame with that elusive little phrase of music, that melody that a woman's voice had sung against, within my own. Devlin appeared at my side, and pulled me by the sleeve, took me by the arm, and led me to a smaller room off the main *salon*, where a merry little fire burned in the grate, and where, in front of another window, with the early evening's light blazing around her, the dark of deep green velvet curtains framing her, stood the woman of the shining hair, the silver voice.

She turned as we entered, and I saw her face. Framed by woven, plaited hair, of a silver-gold colour, her great grey-blue eyes looked frankly at me, humorously. She is very little older than myself, I'd hazard. Her skin is pale, her eyebrows delicate arcs, her lips dark and bitten, purple shadows beneath her eyes, a delicate tracery of blue veins visible around her temples and at her throat. Her clothes are black and dark silver-grey, surely widow's weeds. A silver crucifix, at her throat, and jet beads, perhaps a rosary of sorts, at her wrist, are her only ornaments. Do I dwell more than is proper, Milly, on this woman? Let me say only that I have never seen someone who looked at once so clever, so sad, so beautiful, and whose eyes caused me such a pang of emotion, of what was it? I cannot say. Recognition, strangeness, sympathy, and terror. She was all these things.

Devlin took her hand, and bowed deeply over it, pressed his forehead to it, it seemed, rather than kissing it. "Your talents are surpassed only by your exquisite sensibility, my lady, " he said. "But 'twas not your song, to start with. You only stole it from him." Here, he looked sidelong at me. I was holding to the arm of a couch, in a strange weakness that came over my limbs.

"Sir, " she curtseyed to me, her voluminous black skirts rustling around her. "Your song moved me so. An Irish song? Tell me, what do they mean, those words in Gaelic?"

"You mean, you did not know the song? Excuse me, Madame, I am... speechless. Your accompaniment...your, your descant ..." I stuttered, and stopped. She smiled. Oh!

"I did not know it, but it is a simple melody enough. You sang it so well, so true, it was easy to join you, and easy to help you sing it to a close. Not so, Mr Devlin?"

"Exactly so, my lady. But do, Thomas, do tell us what the lines meant. I have only a little Irish myself, not near enough. It is becoming quite the thing these days, and those of us without are feeling much cut-off from the people and their traditions. You speak it then?" .

"My mother's family spoke it always. She grew up in a small village, on the Iveragh Peninsula. We would spend Summers there, as children."

They both nodded approvingly, and brought me to sit on a couch near the fireplace, where the young lady sat beside me, and settled her skirts around

PART III

her, so that I could feel their rustle along my leg. Devlin pulled a chair to one side of us, and they looked at me expectantly. So I told them what I remember of that song, *Siúil a Rúin*. I write for you too the lyrics here; ask Mama to sing it for you. It's a beautiful, sad song. But a strange one for me to choose, perhaps.

Siúil a Rúin[8]

I wish I was on yonder hill
'Tis there I'd sit and cry my fill
And every tear would turn a mill
Is go dté tú mo mhúirnín slán

Siúil, siúil, siúil a rúin
Siúil go socair agus siúil go ciúin
Siúil go doras agus éalaigh liom
Is go dté tú mo mhúirnín slán

I'll sell my rock, I'll sell my reel
I'll sell my only spinning wheel
To buy my love a sword of steel
Is go dté tú mo mhúirnín slán

I'll dye my petticoats, I'll dye them red
And round the port I'll beg my bread
Until my parents shall wish me dead
Is go dté tú mo mhúirnín slán

I wish, I wish, I wish in vain
I wish I had my heart again
And vainly think I'd not complain
Is go dté tú mo mhúirnín slán

And now my love has gone to France
to try his fortune to advance

---

[8] The last line of each verse may be translated from Irish as 'May you go safely, my darling', and the chorus as 'Go, go my love (*lit.* 'walk'), Go in peace and go in quiet, Go to the door and flee with me, And may you go safely, my darling'. [honestly, Mr Oates, how many of your readers do you think speak Irish? Most emphatically, "STET"]

If he e'er comes back 'tis but a chance
Is go dté tú mo mhúirnín slán

When I told them the meaning of the title, "Go, my love, " or "Walk away, my darling", I said it is a strange word, "rún", for it means "secret" also, and "intention"...and Devlin shook his head and said, "Amazing! Are not there "runes" also in English, come from Norse, and they are secrets both, and signs, signposts of intention, warding, warning ... " It had not occurred to me. The lady said nothing, only sighed. I asked her a question, to fill the silence that came then, asked her what was the instrument she had played. "A cimbalóm, " she said. And suddenly she stood, bobbed quickly to us, whispering "Excuse me, " and she swept from the room.

Devlin stood, went to the fire, and lit a cigar that he had conjured out of nowhere. He smiled at me, most foxy, and asked me what I thought of the *Symboliste* poets. I admitted I hardly knew them, and he began to tell me of some books which he would lend me, strange and wonderful books, oh Milly, how troubling it is, to feel such things, such things hard to speak or to even understand, and these books he has given me, I must confess, when I have read them these last days that I ...

[Thomas MacGilpatrick's letter leaves off here. I found it in a drawer, in his rooms at the Irish College, when I went there after all of the subsequent events were over. It pains me to once more read his tenderness for the young woman, his sister, who shall never now know what became of him. She must not. I wrote to the family, at the time, and I removed all papers, objects, and traces from his chamber, that might link him to any dishonour, or his family. Or link him to us. There were, among his papers, also some other most interesting documents, which I shall come to in time. I wish though, that I could have told the girl, Milly, of her brother's thoughts being with her before the end. She is doubtless grown now, and would rather wish these old wounds not to be re-opened. – W. Crowe]

PART III

PART IV

Devlin's Account of The Long Night

Nov. 1ˢᵗ 1894

So it begins. The Game is underway, the seeds are sown, the dice are cast. And, despite some rotten looking bruises around the face and head, I'll hazard that I'm winning already. Crowe can stuff it in his pipe. He told me, "A full report, Stephen, a full report!"; I said I'd sing it to him if he liked, but he's a man prefers the written word, oh yes, for his accounts, his tallies; he keeps a record in a ledger of all I owe him, and scrupulously writes down his dreams, his readings, his experiments, his bloody bowel-movements for all I know (and I bet they're bloody, now I mention it, for he eats far too frugal fare, full of roughage and bland, saw-dusty Vegetarianist Vileness[1]). So then, off we go, and here we are:

The Ballad of the Long Night, (Being the Adventures of Messrs. Devlin and MacGilpatrick, Out on the Town in Gay Parys, with Assorted Felons, Floozies, and Fabulists, on the Night of Samhain Eve, in this Year of Disgrace 1894).

Dull enough to begin, we were to call on Crowe in his rooms in the Rue du Bac. I dawdled in the courtyard of the Irish College while waiting for Himself, Young Thomas, to make an appearance. Eyed up suspiciously by the Dirty Old Monk, Pierre, who keeps the gate. My, he has a rheumy, squinty Eye! I twandled my ashplant, strolling and whistling, oozing *insouciance* and *je-m'en-foutinɡ* left and right. Some priestly young pale-faces glanced me askance, and I sparked a cigar, the better to make mock at them. I think one strapping young Mayo man would have had at me, when I began to sing *Joy to Great Caesar* soft-loudly to myself. Surprised he knew what I was on about. But they have a nose for Anti-Popery, these little Ultramontane Bookworms. Not a minute soon enough, he arrived, and whisked me off before I could get in any more trouble. Scoldy Thomas,

---

[1] It is none of my concern if you think this may offend your Vegetarian and Vegan readers, Mr Oates. I refuse to edit the text itself to conform to your idea of this vast 'readership' you keep talking about. When was the last time you sold over 100 copies of one of your books, anyway?

chiding me like a child. What larks.

To Crowe's, next. The Crowe's Nest, or Sanctum, is in a dullish stretch of dull aul' street, though I hear the Musketeers once used to drill there. Rue du Bac, D'Artagnan at one end, and the Chapelle de la Medaille Miraculeuse at the other; Crowe, needless to say, favours the Holy, and not the Swashbuckling end. As we entered through the coach-way into the courtyard, a great brute of a man was swinging himself up to the box of a pretty wee rig, two white horses and all. He gave me a grunt and a grudgy tip o' the hat. Fine evening, Abel, I cried. He whipped up his horses, and near ran us down. Thomas, though, I'm sure, caught a good old glimpse in the carriage window as it passed, and saw – a blondey head, and sad blue eyes. Good, good. Her timing is exquisite. Though her lug of a man-servant, Abel Guest, is not one to be tangled with, I'd say. Thomas only looked on as they passed out under the gate. I asked, why the sheepy eyes? He said nothing, only, he thought he saw someone he knew. I know well. Of course he did.

Welcoming us, if you can call it that, Crowe's man Scully took our coats, and my hat and stick, and mumbled that the Master was above, and we were to go right up. Damn but he's a gloomy one! How is it that they all have servants, and not a one is jolly, not a one is comical? Have they seen no Shakespeare, no Molière? If I had servants, I'd employ only gay young blades, and dainty damsels, all ready for a bit of rough-and-tumble, a fight or a flirt, at the drop of a hat. My hat, needless to say. But the question is unlikely to pose itself, as the wages of sin are scanty at best, and allow little margin for the maintaining of a household.
In the sitting-room above, Crowe was waiting in an armchair by the window, a heavy volume on the low lectern by his elbow, seemed to start out of a reverie as we entered. Pshaw, he was waiting. I know, for his window looks down at the approach, and he would have tipped off the young Miss that it was time to be going. Thomas, dubious, asked nothing about her, but they exchanged the pleasantries they are both so attached to. So Crowe must take it up.

"Do you know," he says, "That I have just been speaking of you with a young acquaintance of mine?"

There was a little start from Thomas. Hooked. Well, I may have put her in play, but she's Crowe's piece, really. Wait'll he sees what I have in store, though. He'll

PART IV

soon lose interest in Little Miss Silver'n'Gold. Crowe told him he'd had a Young Lady come to him for advice and instruction. He mentions her and Thomas's meeting a few weeks ago, says she was asking for him, the *futur curé*. Says she wishes she'd had time to talk, hopes she was not rude, is so *pleased* that he's made the acquaintance of Master Crowe now, and wouldn't it be delightful for them both to come to tea with her one of these days, for to continue their most interesting discussions. She's a Seeker after the Truth, Crowe lets drop. She's a Sheep as has Lost her Way, he heavily intimates. She wishes she'd a Faith as strong and sound as yours, Thomas. Thomas, affecting indifference, or polite interest, saunters awkwardly round the room, picking up books he can't see, objects he can't feel. His ears are bright red. Oh-ho now! She's made a hit, there's for sure. Her name? Oh, Crowe goes, Naughty Devlin didn't introduce you? She is Mrs Sophia Walker. Come to Paris for study and rest, after the death of her dear husband, in this Time of Trouble of her Faith. Yes, yes, a Catholic. One can always tell, can't one? I snorted. Crowe glared. He rang for tea.

Scully lit us our way upstairs, and we bypassed the main library, up the narrower winding stair into the tower above. I rubbed my hands in glee, for Crowe has kept me from up here for years. Fears I'll nobble his favourite grimoires, no doubt. I would, it's true, but for their monetary rather than arcane value. How more sorry would he be were I to make off with a treasured incunabulum, only to have it turn up in one of his esoteric book-dealer's lists? Though at least then he could buy it back. Must study this question, for circulation of wealth is a laudable goal, as long as it circulates through my pockets...

Above, in The Hidden Library, Scully busied himself with lighting the thick waxy frozen waterfalls of candles around about, to dispel the gloom of the late afternoon, though watery light filtered through from the glassy dome above us, in the round tower room of this folly. Thomas glanced around politely, but I ran, panting, to the shelves, and ducked side to side like a hound on the scent at the rich fruit of plunder there! His books on alchemy alone, they had me slavering: he had the works of Avicenna, of Lully, of Nicolas Flamel, who, with his wife Pernella, is rumoured still to wander among the Dervish tribes of the desert, the Elixir achieved; he had the *Gháyat al-Hakím fi'l-sihr*, the *Clavicula Salomonis*, an Abramelin; he had the false – and the true – works of Hermes Thrice-Great, displayed in such a way as to show he knew the difference; Agrippa's *De occulta philosophia* was there, with Paracelsus; the great connoisseurs of the Legion

Spirits of the Abyss, Fr. Michaelis and Dr. Dee, alongside the *Daemonolatreia* of Remigius; the herbals of Culpepper, the Inquisition's *Malleus Malleficarum*, and such subtle delvers as Trithemius, Pico della Mirandola, Olaus Wormius, Joachim of Flora, and Qabbalistic confectioneries a-plenty[2]. Oh, but it was a rich and rare collection he had amassed, Old Bill. He took Thomas by the arm, and showed off some of the beautiful illuminated volumes.

The boy's brow furrowed, and he seemed to catch a whiff of the sulphurous nature of the forbidden books sitting blasphemously on the shelves. *Un véritable Enfer!* he exclaimed. Crowe smiled, smugly. Had not Thomas seen such rooms, in his erring in the great libraries of the Vatican? For surely, it was not an innocent the Church was meaning to make of him? Thomas nodded an uncomfortable assent. What *did* they mean to make of him, one wonders? And if they succeeded, would we not find ourselves on opposite sides of a Great Divide? That thought, unspoken, passed between myself and Crowe, with a conspiratorial look.

The stripling's eyes were elsewhere, for he now addressed himself to the study of the objects and curiosities that were set on plinths around the corners of the round room, or in alcoves and niches among the books. A many-breasted Isis, and a leering little Priapus had their places, and he lingered to look close at what – as he soon noticed – was a most Odious Grecian Urn, its men and boys, red on black, engaged in athletic embraces, in the manner of the *symposiasts* of that Grand Epoch. Crowe hurried him away from this one, perhaps wishing to distract him from thoughts of the induction rites of Athenian youths. He displayed with pride his Bell of Saint Patrick – one of the dozens the holy man had made, Crowe said, cast in iron, then dipped in bronze in case men's eyes would be blinded by their sanctity. Stranger still, there was: the mummified head of some unfortunate from the dawntimes, his flesh blackened but preserved by the action of the bog in which he'd fallen, or was thrown.

"Only think!" Crowe cried, transported. "This doughty warrior walked the earth while Moses tended his flocks in Midian, or before ..."

---

[2] Very well. Again, I had thought my footnote a model of scholarly elucidation, but if you're sure that all of your readers will be so well-versed in what you term this 'Occult Bibliography For Beginners', then far be it from me to stick my oar in.

PART IV

Thomas was suitably impressed. I took the opportunity, while their eyes gazed into some legendary past, to slip out a quaintly typeset volume of Rétif de la Bretonne's *Les Nuits de Paris, ou le Spectateur nocturne*, which I had heard was full of *terribly* instructive illustrations, but Crowe darted sideways and snatched it, tutting and clucking over it like it was a darling child who'd had a fall. Wounded, I took my pride off to the other side of the room, and there saw a thing of astounding beauty. I had discussed with Crowe the plans for this table, but this was the first time I had seen the finished product. As I flitted into the tiny side-chapel that contained it, I let whoop a cry of joy, and the others followed me to see this little wonder.

About the size of a billiard table, the surface was of carefully worked hazel-wood, and growing up the middle, a representation of a great branching tree of ash. From its root to its crown, and in sets of branches in between, were discs the size of dinner plates, ten in number, four up the middle, three along each side. Between the discs, were marble paths; around them, runes and symbols, inscriptions, diagrams. Crowe watched me, as I ran my hands along the surfaces, traced the patterns with my fingers. Did it meet with my approval, he asked. I could only sigh. Thomas looked on, puzzlement and wonder in his eyes, and some trace of terror, as if he felt the Trembling of the Veil. What was it, he asked. As Crowe began to speak, the underwater light above was fading, and the candle flames seemed to burn pure and high. I became aware of tumbling blue tendrils of smoke snaking around us, hanging in whorls and clouds below the low ceiling of the alcove: some incense of Crowe's, some powder, ground from fossilised basilisk tears, perhaps; I saw this sweet, heady perfume tumbling from a Byzantine thurible that hung from its chain in another alcove.

"This, my young friend, is the Tree of the Cosmos, the Tree of Life[3]. You might think of it as the Tree of the Knowledge of Good and Evil, the fruit of which, plucked in Eden, has made us Fallen. The Norsemen knew it as Yggdrasil, on which hung the worlds of men, of giants, of elves, of gods. The Jewish mystics, students of the Qabbalah, have named these ten *sephiroth*, the spheres, emanations of God, and traced the paths between them. With Devlin here, and after many years of study, I have combined these, and other cosmologies, to make this that you see before you. Each disc is a symbol, a complex one, in alchemical, theological, and mystical terms. You see here...at the bottom the Stone Circle, Kingdom of the Earth. At the top, there, in gold inlaid with diamond, is the Purest Spirit. Between are the Realms of the Iron King, on the right hand, beneath him

---

[3] [if you insist] See Margery Davenport's *Introduction to the Mysteries of the Tree of Life* (Savage House, 2008).

PART IV

30

lead and lodestone, in the form of the Compass Rose, for wealth and learning, and then yew wood, for the Romance of the Forest. On the left is the Star of the Sea, the Queen of Heaven, her disc of the ivory of a narwhal's tusk, then bronze for the Warrior's Ordeal, and the fire of purification, and then the Labyrinth, of glass and quicksilver, for wit, insight, and science. In the middle, between the Earthly Kingdom, and the High Holy Spirit, there is the Silver Moon, for dreams, and the Brass Sun, where men's lives become the lives of heroes, and where gods die, and are reborn."

The Spheres and Paths seemed to glitter and pulse with the presences of Gods, Daemons, and magical powers, Chthonic and Ouranian. Thomas stared, his eyes drinking thirstily, greedily. He could almost decipher the charged names, could make out the terrible energy that the mere juxtaposition of such symbols and materials creates. Crowe said something to him, in what tongue? Ancient Greek! And Thomas responded, an automatic antiphon, in a sing-song dreamy voice. Blast it! Not fair! Little Latin have I, and less Greek, [4] and Crowe was surely cheating now. These riches, and this learning that they share, the darker learning he *would* share with our young novice. I couldn't have it. We must out.

"Christ's toes!" I sang out. "The pair of you!...One thinks of Homer... Pff! Come, Thomas, let's out of this stuffy study. We're keeping the old bachelor from his dusty books, no doubt, and two young bucks like us, we should be off, we should be out!"

Thomas shook his head, as if waking from a dream. I strode back towards the stairs, chivvying him, harrying him, trying to ignore Crowe's black looks. I'd disrupted his ambiance, and ruined his moment, it seems. All the better.

"Go back to playing with your toys, Sweet William! And damn your Special Table! As *balls* to wanton gentlemen are we to the Gods: they play billiards with our souls!" I cackled and shouted this back over my shoulder, dragging Thomas stumbling in my wake down the narrow winding stair. Crowe called back, crestfallen, that he had been about to show us the playing pieces. Those, on the contrary, I had seen. I knew that he would now set them out, on the

---

[4] I know *you* know the quotation, but some people might not. What do you have against Shakespeare?
[I see. Which one is it then, Francis Bacon or Christopher Marlowe?]

Table of the Tree, mine on the left side, his on the right. I knew that he would put in play four pieces, three at *Malkuth*, the Kingdom of the Earth, the Beginning: his piece, the Knight of Pentacles, with his scholar's robes, and book and bell; my piece, the Knight of Wands, of Wanderers, which we had fashioned with a vagabond's staff and a minstrel's harp; Thomas's piece, the Knight of Cups, the Grail Knight, the poor doomed would-be Galahad, preparing to be tested. And at the Disc of the Moon, at *Yesod*, there would be the Silver Maiden, for he had played her as his opening. The Board will change tonight, I told myself, oh yes!

I strode out smartly, pulling Thomas along behind me. We must work fast, I told him, for the sun's near down, and the Long Night about to begin.

Oh, swift we sniffed the evening air, the dying day, as I felt that tingle of anticipation that one has, when devilry's afoot, and when the pockets brim with gold (of Crowe's, of course), and the City lies spread out before one's feet!
We hurried past the pale and cringing crowds that were beginning to gather outside the Church of Saint-Germanus-in-the-fields, preparing to pray for the safety of their souls on this Hallowmass Eve, and on, to the Carrefour de l'Odéon. Thomas drifted behind me, his eyes on far-off things. I tried to snap him out, with talk and chat, and jokes and tales, but I could feel Crowe's grip tighten, even at this distance. We would step sideways, then, I suggested, and pause, for it was beginning to be *l'heure bleu*, and it was time. The day dripped away, as the sky fell from us, and the fathomless deeps of blue opened up. Above the city streets, where the gas lamps began burning, the Heavens glowed with mystery. A sliver of the New Moon rose above the serried roofs, and tobaccos and perfumes mingled with the earthy hum of mouldering fallen leaves and putrefaction. Come with me, Gentle Sir, I sang to him, and follow, and I'll show you the first precious blooms of the City of Dreadful Night. He followed.

Ducking down an alleyway, under an arch and along the cobbles, we came to a little place I know, under the sign of the Crescent Moon and Troubadour. Thomas looked around him. He said he'd never seen the street before. He had not looked, I told him. Shall we? I offered him my arm, but he was not convinced, so I pushed the door of the little tavern, and sure enough, he followed. Inside, there was roaring at the zinc bar, and a great beast of a man polishing glasses, his roar loudest over all. Students in shapeless hats blew clouds of smoke from dirty little pipes, and artists in stained smocks ribbed each other, laughed and told grand lies about their bright futures. With them sat their models and their muses, so deliciously just-dressed, so terribly liable to slip right back out of the slovenly clothes thrown on. The *serveuses*, buxom beauties, or sylphlike slips of girls, twirled trays between laden tables. A cackling hag gummed at a great clay pipe at her table in the corner, while around her men in shirt-sleeves sweated over their hands of cards. *Henri! Deux absinthes, mon vieux!* I picked up a young poet by his ear, and shooed him and the English painter he was attempting to shake down for a few francs away from my table in the window.

"So what do you think, Thomas the Dubious, of our first stop of the night? *La Lune d'Orphée*, they call it. Ah, here's Henri with a little sip of something to set your mind at unrest ..."

Thomas didn't speak, but looked around him now with more attention. A lively, gay young crowd. I saw it in him, the same look I've seen poor William give, when he finds himself amidst carousing, cursing, living, breathing men and women. A lost and lonely look. The look of a small boy starving, as he stares through the window of the cake-shop, as he dawdles on his way to lessons. They bury their heads in their Virgil then, poor scholars, as if being put to the top of the class will make up for the hunger, and the taunts. Ah, rather be in my gang, the bold fellows who will go off miching from school, swipe the sweets from the counter when the lady isn't looking, dash in the streets, and fish in the rivers, bribe the girls with toffees to let us look under their skirts ...

"Now first, Thomas, you must savour the occasion. A sugar-lump upon the spoon, thus, that rests across the top of the glass, thisways. Now we pour the water...tinkle, twinkle, tum. See how it clouds the liquor, see how jewelly amber turns to cloudy green! Your turn. Absinthe makes the heart grow fonder, did you know? Makes the mind grow keener, makes the spirit sing; you'll see! *La fée verte*, lightly stepping here among us... See who else around us is partaking. Look! Now see the way their eyes shine in reverie, and their pipe-smoke trickles up and makes blue clouds around their heads to represent their dreams? Yes. Drink! Drink up! *Henri! Deux autres, s'il te plait!* You'll see."

He downed the rest of his glass, and murmured *semper in absentes felicior aestus amantes*, or words to that effect. I concurred.

PART IV

"You see this room around you, Thomas? You see this low dive, these seedy scholars, the cheap little *grisettes*, underdressed, underfed, the morose poets with their droopy beards? Would it surprise you to know that Beauty also is here? That Glory is not unknown, that Joy alights here – more often, perhaps, than in places you frequent?"

"I *do* see," he nodded, earnest now, the flush of his cheeks and the shine of his eyes betraying the beginnings of Effect. "They are beautiful, in their laughter, in their camaraderie. But this place is filled with a host of Occasions of Sin. There are traps for the unwary here."

He sat back in his chair, and took another sip from his refilled glass, then looked at it suddenly, and put it down. A plump, pretty-ish girl, with over-curled hair, sidled up to our table. *Vous voulez qu'on se prenne un p'tit verre ensemble, les amis?* I waved her off. Thomas looked on mildly. Be not forgetful to entertain strangers, he told me, for thereby some have entertained angels unaware. Yes, yes, certainly. But I say, let the angels entertain *me*, not the other way around, and I'll treat them to all the drinks they like. She looked like a grasping whiny type. No, we'll do much better than that tonight, you mark my words.

We sipped, and slurped, and I smoked a cigarette, one of the special ones I had made, the last time I was in funds, from finest Turk tobacco, with a little something Moroccan in admixture, just to take the edge off. The laughter and the shouts of *la vie de bohème* around us seemed to fade, then rise again, as the blue smoke drifted and the fairy green in the bulb of the absinthe glasses twinkled, then clouded, then twinkled anew. Thomas looked on, and I watched him look. Dreaminess began to set in, and I saw his eye come clear and shining, and his heart begin to cloud with trouble. Time to move. I slapped down two ringing coins upon the table, and pulled him to his feet. Off, off we go, for time's a-wasting! Onwards and upwards!

As we pushed through braying crowds along the bar, I saw his eyes twist, stop, then break away. I looked back from the door, as he pushed past me, into the cool and smoky evening air. I knew what he'd seen, for I saw it too: a small and slender woman at the bar, with green-blonde hair like river-weeds, turned her eyes on me, and her pupils in their golden, feline orbs were vertical slits. From her shoulders, for a moment, in the shimmering light, there spread a delicate pair of jewelled dragonfly wings. I chuckled, for if he could see *that* already, then my work was halfway done. She never blinked, but raised a glass to me of ruby nectar, and I tipped my hat her way, and left.

"What do you mean by bringing me to such a place?" he puffed, striding to keep up as I tore off through the narrow streets that would lead us to the Seine.

"You must meet *all* your future flock, *n'est-ce pas*? And know, Young Master Thomas, that there are those that walk the Earth who never will fall under your authority, should you become a priest. Tonight of all nights, they're abroad."

He never answered, but kept pace, and we made it to the Fontaine Saint-Michel, where the poor Archangel Michael cowers, his flaming sword extinguished, as the Devil rises in triumph behind him, covering him in the shadow of his outstretched dragon-wings. One of Baron Huysmans's greater efforts, I've always thought. Crossing to the Quai, we strolled now, slower, and passed across the Petit Pont in the shadow of the Hôtel-Dieu. From high narrow windows, there drifted the stench of illness, and the thin wails of lunatics. Beyond that grim infirmary, one could see rising the blackened mass of Notre-Dame. A dark cathedral, and little comfort. He crossed himself. Don't be troubled, said I, for tonight they'll think they're free, and their war-torn minds declare a truce, their wearied souls lay down in greener pastures. Tonight, all changes; nothing is, but what is not. You'll see. He did not see. Blessed are those who have not seen, and yet still believe. My mission is to make him *see*.

On the Parvis, in front of Notre-Dame, fine folk hurried out as the last murmurs of the Mass declined, ran the gauntlet of the beggars and the false-war-wounded, the trembling urchins and the skipping lame, the sharp-eyed blind. The Cour des Miracles swarmed with members of the Argot-Guild of Vagabonds. Before the Lady's Temple, the pillory and the gibbet rose, with three ripe corpses on the one, and a whimpering young girl tied to the other, her tattered rags scarce covering her raw-flogged back. Some filthy, snotty children tried to approach her, crust of bread and cup of bitter wine held out, but a soldier of the Royal Watch cracked his whip and sent them running.

PART IV

"You see the scaffold, and the gibbet, Thomas dear? *This* is the very centre of France. From here are all the roads to Paris measured. But I'm sure you knew that."

"Blessed are the poor, in spirit, " he muttered, "for the Kingdom of Heaven...belongs to them."

"And the meek, Thomas?" A girl-child, holding an infant almost as big as herself, stood before us, whispering entreaties or enchantments. "What shall be left, for them to inherit, when the proud have done with it? Come, much more to see."

I flipped a coin at the girl, and she dropped the child to jump and catch it. As he hit the ground and wailed, the girl was engulfed in a scrambling mass of scrawny limbs and filthy rags, as the murderous Poor trampled a child to get to the flash of gold. Thomas started forward, but I restrained him. Look! The child was toddling off rapidly, in his hands a bright gold coin; the girl squirmed out from the scrimmage, laughing, and left them to fight, while she swept the child in her arms and ran.

Across another bridge, where a piper skirled a merry tune, and rough apprentice-boys danced with girls in red-dyed petticoats, no better than they should be, we wandered down the length of the Ile-Saint-Louis, to the end, and crossed the right arm of the river, to the Quai of the Celestials. Here, the shop-fronts bustled with bright silks and pig-tails, as chicken feet, strange herbs and spices and steaming noodles were handed across crowded counters. Here, we must hurry by, for this is only a night like any other, to the Chinaman, who sits smoking his long pipe beneath the lanterns of coloured paper, with snaking golden dragons coiled above him; here, we are briefly in the influence of other Powers, and other Realms, and the Long Night of Samhain means nothing, and alien eyes follow the two of us as we walk. Again, he's never been here, Thomas. I wonder what must he do with his time. Study, he tells me. Ah.

We crossed the hurrying thoroughfare of Rivoli, and to our right, at the far end of the street, loomed the great turreted shadow of the Bastiglia di Sant'Antonio,

dwarfing the poor column in front of it, where a sad gold "Mercury, or, the Spirit of Liberty", is frozen in the act of taking flight; he is a mocking commemoration of the Failed Rebellion of '89. Over a century later, Italian troops sent by the Pope still guard the eastern approach to the city, and the Bastiglia stands as a warning to any who would trifle with the King. But there we must not go, tonight, for the Chaplain of the Bastiglia is well-known to me, and I have no wish to cross him. No, we shall run to the Rue des Rosiers, for it is time to eat.

PART IV

It is not only the good Christians who are hurrying home to bolt their doors against the gathering dark; here, the Chasidim of the Jewish Quarter know the meaning of this feast, for they have lived in Poland, in Ukraine, in Hungary, and know how the Old Bargain works. Men in long black coats, with beards and sidelocks, hurry to shut up their shops, and strike for home; the women and the children are already gone from the streets. Thomas looked in wonder at the Hebrew lettering of the signs, at the six-pointed stars in the windows. I led him to a door, and knocked.

The door was pulled open a crack, and then flung wide. Its frame was filled by an enormous bear of a man, his beard spilling down to his waist. He blocked the light of candles beyond, and glared at us. I took off my hat, and bowed. "Schön guten Abend, Dov ben Hakim!" German was the closest I could do with him. "Blessings on your Household, on this Night of Nights." He sighed, and motioned us past him into the house, looking both ways in the street before slamming shut the door once more, and locking it. Within, a small hearth held a sputtering fire, and at a rough table, a pale, tired, dark-eyed woman rose suddenly, on seeing us enter. Her hand flew to the head of a little boy, who sat before his plate, expectant. On the wall behind them, was a spray of woven palm leaves, boughs of myrtle, branches of willow, and the citrus fruit.[5]

"Set two more Places for the Evening-meal, Eszter, love, " the man grumbled in Yiddish. "We have Guests." His wife shot me a murderous glance.

And then – wonders will never cease, of course – Young Thomas surprised us all, for he bowed to them, and, touching his hand to the wall below the little scroll-case affixed to the door-frame, he murmured "*Barukh atah Adonai Eloheinu melekh ha-olam, asher kideshanu bemitzvotav vetzivanu likboa' mezuzah*". Dov and Eszter looked at him, and at me, in puzzlement. Thomas came into the room, and asked them forgive us for our intrusion during one of the nights of the Feast of Ingathering. In Hebrew! Clever, clever boy. I felt quite the dullard. I nudged him, and he told me what he'd said. I took him up, and said to them it

---

[5] What happened to the last FIVE pages of notes? I worked extremely hard on those! It is impossible to accurately follow the progress of Devlin and Thomas across Paris if one knows nothing of Baron Huysmans's renovation of Paris, for example. Is it not even *slightly* interesting to know he was the father of JK Huysmans, whose novels so clearly influenced this one? And the parallels between the Jewish Feast of Sukkot and the Celtic Harvest Festival of Samhain, I would have thought, were very enlightening. I'm seriously starting to question the wisdom of working with you. This is unacceptable. [PS The last expenses cheque bounced. Just so you know]

was a happy chance, that tonight that Feast did coincide with our own, the *Oíche Shamhna* of Summer's End, the Long Night. Esther took Thomas to sit between her and her husband at the head of the table, for she said he must be a holy man. I squeezed in at the foot, against the wall, and looked daggers at the little boy, who had his eye on my small portion of the fare.

We ate in silence, after Thomas had joined Dov to say the prayers. The small family looked at me, their eyes clouded with hate. Thomas asked the name of the boy, but Eszter shushed him, said we must not say, this Night of all Nights, and we call him "Alter", only. Thomas bowed his head, and said a brief prayer for the Innocent Dead, and Dov's eyes brimmed with long-unshed tears. They will not speak their son's name aloud, for fear he may be taken also, as his brothers and his sisters were before. I would have offered them my sympathy, had I thought they'd take it, but our dealings have been bitter, and Dov ben Hakim owes me an old, old debt, which he will pay, and pay, until the time runs out. Dov refused my hand in parting. He was the one who incurred the debt. I will not forget it, for I must keep my tallies straight as well, even as Crowe does, though mine are written in secret ledgers of the heart.

We left them there, and the door slammed after us. Thomas was quiet, and I led him through the quieter streets. The last doors were closing, the lamp-light furtive behind the shutters. I strode on, swinging my stick. He wandered after me, looking around, his eyes raised to the darkened, narrow buildings on either side, leaning in over us, looming. I turned to him, at a gloomy corner, and asked him why he dawdled. He had never seen the streets of Paris at night, he told me, and had never walked through these winding lanes at all. I am here to remedy this lack, I said.

As we approached, it's hard to say which reached us first, the smell – of rotting vegetable matter, foul fish, broken meats – or the sound of the tolling bell. It clanged a strident, yellow note, that rang around the echoing, empty streets. Closer now, and the sibilant scurryings in the corners, in the shadows, in the mouths of doorways and behind pillared arcades, began to gather, and the movements at the edge of vision multiplied. Thomas stuck close to me, trying to make out the shapes that followed our steps, trying to discern the fleeing silhouettes between the buildings that emerged and joined the dark stream of

PART IV

ghosts in whose midst we walked. The bell still tolled its broken summons, and the broken People of the Bell limped and loped, staggered and sidled towards the Belly of the Beast.

"You see these, Thomas? They're the *Clochards*, the walking-wounded of the city. They're the limping lame, *clopin-clopant*, the bell-ringing, bell-answering masterless men. They're being called to supper. But look, pass quickly. We're in the shadow of the Tower."

On the square, bright gas-beak-lamps lit up the scene, but the rabble passing with us fled up sidestreets, for in front of the Torre de Santiago, and the Church of Saint-James-the-Son-of-Thunder, there was a procession, bearing torches all, and banners, to the thump of muffled drums. Their robes were black, and bore, as did their banners, the red cross *fleury fitchy*, its lower branch terminating in a sword-blade. Thomas stopped, reverently, and bowed his head. I tugged his sleeve, but he put a finger to his lips, and pointed at the coffin being carried by six men, draped also in the standard of the Knights of Santiago. He joined his hands, and moved his lips in prayer. I started, for at once there was a third one standing with us, and I knew him. Also in black robes, but his a rusty, threadbare black, he stood no taller than myself, but twice as wide, with thick black curling hair, a bristling, wiry beard, and a broad, dark smiling face. He winked at me, and bowed his head as well, while the gentlemen went by. Across his body, crooked between his joined hands and against his shoulder, he held a tall staff, twice his height, with a hook at the bottom, and a wick on the top. In his satchel, there would be the powders, tinder-box, spare wicks, candles, and the vials of phosphor of his trade, or duty, what you will. The procession passed within the gates of the church, and a hollow, echoing chanting began within.

"So! Stefano Hechizado[6], you introduce me to your friend?" the fat monk said.

"Go away, Hiedra. We're busy." I took Thomas's arm, and made to walk off. But Fra Hiedra followed. He said he was on his rounds, and would accompany us as far as the Cimetière des Innocents, if we didn't mind waiting

---

[6] Spanish : Accursed. Possibly a translation of the Irish version of Devlin, Dobhailein, 'the unfortunate'. Whether this might be linked to 'diabhal', devil – 'bedevilled' is unclear.

as he worked, from time to time. Thomas, of course, became interested, and I could but sigh. The tolling of the bell had died now, and my *coup de théâtre* was deflated. Nonetheless, if Hiedra didn't dawdle too long, we'd make it to Les Halles on time. Besides, it was perhaps as well to walk along the walls and see the portals of Les Innocents. I ought to have thought. Most fitting. Hiedra was explaining, with much bragging, of his oh-so-symbolic *métier*. I am the Lightbearer[7], the Lamplighter, he said, Carrier of the Torch in Darkness; I go from Santiago's Tower each night, and I light the streets, and light the way to lost souls, where I find them. I light the candles of the church, and hold the lantern as the pilgrims set out before the dawn, I pin the Scallop badge to their coats, and show them their road. He is an oily, self-satisfied dago, I've always thought. And he would do well to keep his titles and his deeds to himself.

Every so often, Hiedra would pause – still talking, mind you – and deftly spark the wick on the end of his long staff, then dart it upwards, unerring, to the dark glass of a gas-beak. With a twist, the catch was clicked, and a whoosh, the lamp flared up. As the streets became even darker, and narrower, he attached a small lantern to his staff, on a hook halfway up, where it hung above our heads, as he bore it like a lance against his shoulder. Here and there, we'd pass a little counter where a light still burned, where cabmen and streetwalkers drank a miserable coffee, or a little mug of wine. They hailed Hiedra, and he ostentatiously blessed them as he passed.

"You see, Tomás," droned Hiedra, "the poor, the sick, the sinners. These are *my* flock. To them I bear the Light of Christ in Darkness. These are the Noctambules, the Night-Court. They must have their ministers too. *Hé, obrigado, filho!*" He patted a child on the head, who'd run from a meagre little wine-vendor's stall, and presented him with a flask of Porto. He swigged long from it, and offered it to Thomas to taste. I cantered after them, for a warming sup was worth listening to his drivel for.

Ahead, we saw the great south portal of the Cimetière des Innocents, where doubtless all these denizens of the Night-time would end their spell on Earth. Here, the great fresco of the *Danse Macabre* showed the multitudes of men and

---

[7] Thanks for the suggestion, but I'm quite sure that a) *Our Readers* know what Lucifer means, and that b) it is in this case ENTIRELY irrelevant.

PART IV

women, of all stations, and all trades, of the nobles as of the paupers, following the footsteps of the dancing, grim-grinning Angel of Death.[8] Skull-headed imps flocked round them, with their scythes and sickles, and the Pale Horseman followed behind, with his long cruel sword. Below, there were portrayed the torments of Hell, in whose noisome pits howling souls were torn apart for ever, by horned, writhing demons, where dark fire surged from lakes of brimstone, and the rotting corpses of still-conscious sinners were baled high by sturdy devils wielding pitchforks, or tridents, and scourges for the lashing of a lingering, Hell-bound soul. Hiedra waved his fat hand at it all, and pointed out with relish some of the more esoteric tortures. Of course, I know he has as little fear of Hell as I, and is almost as great a sinner. We went on. On the other side of the walled-in cemetery, Hiedra briefly pointed out the sculptured Portal of Nicholas Flamel, great benefactor of the Poor of Paris, and particularly this charnel-house, where the soil consumed their flesh, and then the walls held their bones to dry, when they were dug up to make way for more. There was Old Nick, and Pernella, kneeling both in front of a figure of the Risen Christ, flanked by SS Peter and Paul, and surrounded by the symbols of the Wingèd Lion, the Avenging Angel, the Last Trump, the Dragons Locked in Combat, and other symbols whose alchemical value was plain to see to those who looked. How he got away with that, I'll never know, the heretical old hypocrite. But then, show the Church your money, and you can have whatever you damned-well like erected in your honour. Hiedra raised the lantern to the bas-reliefs, saying Flamel was a good man, though misguided. Some fellow-feeling there, no doubt.

The stench of fish, flesh, fowl, all putrefying, and of root, and leaf, and fruit all a-rot that now assailed us was near overpowering. We arrived at the Great Halls of Paris as the last of the straggling *clochards* were fleeing, with their poor haul clutched tight in their arms. Though I knew that there were young and old among them, they seemed all bent beneath countless years, shrivelled by the light of unforgiving suns, soiled by the filth of squalid suffering. Ambulant bundles of rags, scrawny, sore-spattered limbs, cowering, craven faces flitted past, beneath the great galleries of glass and iron, through the wreckage left over after the close of trade: of broken pallets, empty stalls, strewn straw and sawdust, and excrement and effluvia of every earthly kind.

---

[8] Fine. I won't even try then. As you say, it 'speaks for itself'.

There now began to toll a hand-bell, this one a harsher, thinner, jangling, then another, and another, and the shouts of the Royal Night Guard went up. Hiedra hissed, and handed the lantern to Thomas to hold, then went and stood in the middle of one of the aisles, between the great wrought-iron pillars that held up the arches of the echoing, vaulted roof of shadows. A small flock of feral children, half-naked and carrying bulging sacks across their shoulders, streamed past Fra Hiedra, nearly knocking us aside. Him, they avoided, flowed around, while he planted his feet firmly, and gripped his great lance with both hands. The twangling bells came closer, and two Guardsmen stomped around the corner, shouting, *Courrez! Courrez, Vermines!* Hiedra barred their way. One of the guards laughed, and twirled his moustaches, greeting Hiedra by name. *Dégage, Moineau!* he sneered: be off, little monk, little sparrow. The other guard unlimbered his wicked iron-and-leather scourge, and let it twirl, then *crack!* Hiedra looked behind him, at the fleeing children, then at us. You go your way, el Hechizado. I am most pleased to meet you, Tomás. Let me here to deal with these old *amigos* of mine. You have far to go, *adiós!*

There were two more Royal Guardsmen coming running now, as the one who'd spoken rang a shrill, long warning on his bell, and drew his sabre. Hiedra was rummaging in his bag with one hand, while the other braced his candle-staff for their charge. We're off, I cried, and half-pushed, half-dragged Thomas off down a narrow path between mountains of broken crates. Running feet and shouts were all around, and we dashed through the echoing halls of the abandoned market, slithering on gore and offal underfoot, the light of Hiedra's little lamp swinging crazily, loosing vast, hideous shadows all around us.

Rounding a corner, we almost plunged headlong into a jogging troop of Night Guards. Thomas stopped me with an outstretched arm, and we let them hurry past: these were not mere bell-guards on their rounds, but Royal Fusiliers, rifles at their shoulders, in their yellow jackets with black trim. Poor Old Hiedra, I thought, and absent-mindedly kicked a tin bucket. Thomas gasped in horror, and the Guardsmen stopped, and looked round. Bloody Hell! I looked at my poor walking-stick, wondering how it would fare against bullets and sabres. Thomas held the lantern in both hands before him, as if it would help. The squadron started towards us, when two things happened: first, a sharp whistle

PART IV

to the left, and a beckoning hand, from between the leather hangings at the back of a stinking fish-stall; next, and rather more impressively, a boom, and then a plume of smoke and flame went up from the next hall down, where we had left Hiedra. Take care of himself, indeed. Little did they think he'd the makings of combustion, pyrotechnics, and conflagration in that little frelampier bag of his! The Guards looked round, and Thomas and I skedaddled into the fishmonger's stall, and through the leather curtains. A guttural voice hissed this way, and we took to our heels after the short figure in a long coat, who ran down a sort of hidden alleyway between the backs of stalls and sheds, along a wooden gangway under which a muddy, bloody stream flowed in a ditch.

We passed out through a tiny narrow passage, piled high with refuse, scuttling with rats, and emerged, none the worse but for the filth on our boots and around the skirts of our coats, on the Rue Saint-Dionysius, where gas-lamps blazed once more, ruddy stains against the fog that was falling through the damp air. Our rescuer turned, and bowed, sweeping off his shapeless hat.

"At your service, Gentlemen, " he said, with a crooked grin. "Konstantin Belovuc. And who are you then?" He spoke passable English, with a low, guttural accent, given extra whistles by the broken teeth his smile disclosed. He was a short, stocky boy, with a pale, ill-favoured face, hair cropped to stubble, ears standing out from his round, blunt head. His eyes were narrow, and his leering lips were marred by a scar that snaked across them, and up one cheek. He wore a capacious greatcoat, of indeterminate colour. A likely lad, no doubt.

"Thomas MacGilpatrick." He extended his hand, which the little Hun took, after wiping his own on his coat. "And this is Stephen Devlin. We're from Ireland. We didn't know that – "

"Ach, they never know. I was in the Halle, and I thought I may rob you. But then the Guards... No friends of mine. So then, we're friends, yes? And you must be thirsty, after the running, eh?"

I glanced at Thomas, who looked shaken and pale, much sobered by this last escapade. Well. We'd have to see to that. Perhaps it was all the better. This state of enervation could only help my plans. To the next phase, then, I thought. And if this mannikin thought to accompany us, well, no worse. I flipped him a coin, which he caught, and bit, then squirrelled away beneath his coat. Would he care to walk with us, to our next port of call, I wondered. If there were a mug of something foamy at the end of it, or two? Perhaps a bite to eat? He grinned again, and lifted up the left side of his coat. Beneath, hung from a cunning strap below his left armpit, so it was concealed by the fall of the coat, was a leather scabbard, with a basket-hilted sword inside.

"There's worse, to walk with, than myself. Come, *gospoda*, I walk your way. Stand on my left-hand. No harm will come. My word on this."

Down the Rue Saint-Dionysius, the Night-Court bustled. Pale, trembling sinners, affecting nonchalance, eyed up the bunches of ripe ladies who gathered beneath each gas-lamp, who dawdled in doorways, and who hung from windows above, bare shoulders, powdered cheeks, lacquered curls, all glowing in the soft light from behind them, in their perfumed dens. Thomas cast a cold eye over all. These loose ladies would not tempt him, but then, I knew as much. Not so, young Konstantin. He whistled and waved, and threw out lewd suggestions, blew kisses at the ladies as we passed. I breathed a satisfied sigh. I felt much calmed now, among the *Filles de Joie*, passing by the shysters with their game of Find-the-Lady. Back among my own people, hey! And the boy-brigand had a point: I had quite a thirst.

I sent Konstantin into a shady little *épicerie* with a coin, and he came out with a rotgut two-sous bottle of *eau de vie*, and no change. We uncorked it on the spot, and passed it back and forth, wincing. Thomas, hesitant at first, was prevailed upon to have a swig, which had him gasping, and he took another one to chase the first. Good man. I handed out some cigarettes. Again, the Dubious Priestling demurred, but I lit him one and passed it, and unthinking politeness got the better. That made him choke too, and called for another slug of booze, but then he smoked it alright. The brute-child sucked at his with much gusto, holding the smoke in his lungs before blasting it in a great gasp above. He knew that taste, by all appearances. Whatever the case, I think it did us all a power of good, and the wandering lads and lassies of the Street of Sainted Sin soon seemed fine and gentle folk, to our mollified minds. Drunken hussies spilled out of dives lit by sputtering candles stuck on filthy wine casks. A racing gang of urchin pickpockets once came near us, but a snarl from Konstantin, and a flash of a few

PART IV

inches of blade under his flipped-back coat had them running off for softer prey.

The further up the street we walked, the more candid the invitations from the doorways became, until a pale, shapely creature wearing nothing but a sheet, sitting languorously in a ground-floor windowsill arrested my and Konstantin's attention. Behind her, a tall, thin Madame, all in tight red velvet, came and displayed her to us, extending a rounded arm, pulling down the sheet to show a milk-white breast. She twisted the girl's face towards us, and I saw her dreamy eyes saw nothing, her slow movements were absent and floating. We strolled on. Thomas strode purposefully, his eyes on the cobblestones, his cheeks flaming. The little Hun and I nudged each other, and pointed out particular peaches, gave a whistle now and then at a flash of stocking, or a pair of harridans locked in a lascivious embrace on a balcony above.

But all too soon, it was over, and we were at the Boulevard de l'Annonciation, and the great Archway of Saint-Dionysius, his legend spelled out in its carved panels: his arrival as missionary to the Parisii, his capture and torture by the Lutecian Romans of the Left-Bank, their handing him over to the Gauls, whose Druids pronounced his death, whose wild Priestesses beheaded him, upon which he is said to have picked up his head, washed it in a fountain, and proceeded to tuck it under his arm and run all the way to Montmartre, *mons mercurei et mons martis*, where the bloody Priestesses caught him up, and in their ecstasy tore him limb from limb, and scattered his remains about the temples of the Old Gods Mercury and Mars, on that holy hill. Seems strange to me, to base their sanctity on the extremity of their suffering, these Christian Saints; though Dionysius himself has always struck me as quite a character. The severed head sang psalms as he fled from the Gaulish Maenads, an image that I find irresistibly comic.

Thomas lingered at the Portal, which is indeed grand, but Konstantin, no longer distracted by the Beauties-for-Hire, began to clamour for beer. I quite agreed. There is a little place I know, I told them, and we'd do well to repair there, post haste, for the night was getting chillier, and foggier by the moment. I sparked a Lucifer, and held it to Hiedra's lantern once again, and we passed out through the Portal, to the hinterland of the False-Town beyond. Here the roads were even muddier, and the gas-lamps further apart. We'd passed beyond Hiedra's quarter, beyond the Walls of the Ancien Régime. Here the high buildings were half-finished, or falling into ruins, with no state of good repair between. At one crossroads, where to the left, down the passages, the horse-traders keep their stinking stables, we passed a poor fire in a broken barrel, round which some draggled souls gathered. A Gypsy fiddled and some hands half-clapped. Without the walls, your hearth must be laid out by fire and song only. Poor comfort, this night, when all good folks lock their doors. But our next port of call was near, and there all comforts could be had, for those who could pay, or knew how to ask.

Before one reaches the grim battlements of the Prison Saint-Lazare, on the opposite side of the street, there is a gaily-lit entrance, where some gaudy

P.

Jezebels linger in the lamplight. They stand beneath the sign of The Mermaid, and bid lonely travellers welcome. I have seen them jeer and call at the stern nuns who hurry to the Prison, to do their duties there, the Sisters of Saint-Joseph-de-Lyon, who minister to the poor fallen women in that gloomy house of correction. The ladies brazenly wave their cards at the nuns, to show their fully paid-up dues, to show they are not of the sad cohort of the *insoumises*, the Lost Girls, orphans and unregistered whores, or those too sick in mind or body to pass the medical inspection. The ladies of La Sirène, on the other hand, are plump and well-fed as house-cats, for their Mistress knows how to take care of a girl. They purred at my approach, and took my hands, and kissed my cheeks. *Soyez les bienvenus*, they told us, to the Cabaret de la Sirène. The show is just about to begin. The show is *always* just about to begin, isn't it, *mes chéries*, I laughed, and led my two associates inside beneath the lamp.

Thomas took my arm, and said no, what kind of place is this? We should not be here, he insisted. Where else do you see a warm welcome, and a chance to rest and wet our whistle, I asked. Would you have us go back out into the fog? Take our chances with the cut-throats, or the Night-Guards? Thomas hesitated, then shrugged and followed, a little unsteady on his feet, and we passed through the vestibule, into the great room beyond. There, the laughter and the music, the smells of warmth and wine, and sweat burst upon us. The tables were all crowded tonight, and I greeted one or two familiar faces as we passed between them.

La Belle Charlotte greeted me with a kiss, and looked my companions up and down, then led us to a table. I shouted for beer and soup, and smacked her on her juicy rump as she turned to go. She giggled, and waved a finger at me. *Monsieur sera puni, s'il ne fait pas attention*! We can but hope, I told Thomas and Konstantin. The Irish lad, if he thought we'd been in a house of sin at *La Lune d'Orphée*, must have then felt we'd reached its very wellspring. All around us, a mix of gentlemen and ruffians, drinking, smoking, dandling young ladies in their laps; the girls were out in force, mingling from table to table, cuddling and flirting with the men who looked like they had the means. Here indoors, where the heat of the fire and the raucous crowd hung in a fug above us, many of them had dispensed with all but the merest of garments. A light chemise, a petticoat. A red-headed, lynx-eyed beauty to our left wore a sort of filmy stole, that wrapped around her body and over one shoulder, held in place by a brooch and a belt, but disguising none of her lithe charms. Konstantin was rapt, though when the soup, bread, and beer arrived, he fell to with gusto. Thomas sipped his beer, and shot me a look of mute reproach.

A merry air was struck up by the little bony tortoise-headed pianist. Two tasty girls then strolled upon the stage, these dressed in tight-fitting versions of the garb of a fashionable young dandy, trousers and well-cut waistcoats, neatly *décolleté*, little dainty versions of top-hats. They swung their jackets on their shoulders, showing their arms and shoulders to be bare, and made a pantomime of meeting, of offering and taking a cigarette and lighting it, and then of flirting in the most exaggerated and suggestive manner, and one began a serenade to the other, a song of quite frank obscenity, dressed in the most witty word-play and slang. I was quite taken with the performance, and found the conceit of these two girl-boys playing at courting most to my taste. While my eye was elsewhere, I did not spot the group that came and occupied the table next to us, until one of them poked me in the shoulder, with the silver top of a cane.

"*Mais Devlin, c'est vous!*" he shrieked. "Where have you been, *mon cher*? Our *soirées* have not been the same! Oh, but excuse me, who are the two *gallants garçons*? Present us, immediately!"

He was an aging exquisite, with teased, curled hair, dyed dark, and the trace of fard upon his cheeks. His little *bande de folles* gathered round him, simpering and smirking, whispering behind their delicately-manicured hands. One of them, with sly, womanish eyes, slunk around the old *roué*'s shoulder, and draped himself there, grimacing at me.

"Do I owe you money at the moment, Cagliostro?" I barked (for that was the name he had adopted, with veiled allusions to his links to its earlier pseudonymous bearer). He made a little *moue* of deprecation, and I went on, "Then leave me to enjoy my evening, and tell your little fauns to keep their snouts to themselves!"

One of the perfumed prancers had sidled over to our table, and made some gesture and murmur to Thomas, who gazed steadfastly away (though where to look, he could scarce decide). Konstantin stood suddenly, soup dribbling still down his chin, wiped a sleeve across his face and in the same gesture smartly

PART IV

smashed an elbow in the little *chéri*'s face. He squawked, and fell back among his solicitous coterie, hands to his blood-bursting, swelling nose. Cagliostro waved a hand, and put a scented lace kerchief to his nose. Charlotte reappeared immediately, for there was a slight stir around us, and some young swells at another table were jumping to their feet, and taking the measure of Konstantin, who looked around, and growled, and put his hand beneath his coat, to I-knew-where.

"Monsieur Devlin, hold him on the leash, your hound, " she ordered, smiling gracefully all around her. "For tonight, then, have you decided? *Vous montez, ou vous descendez?*"

"What's it to be, my lusty lads, eh?" I grasped Konstantin and Thomas by the arms. "Shall we up, or shall we down?"

"I'd get up on her, in an eye-blink, " the hound-boy muttered, wiping his mouth again, and licking his chops. Charlotte smiled enticingly, and told him no, *chéri*, she had other business to attend to, but she would be sure to have him well taken care of, if he wished. He downed the rest of his mug of beer, and said as long as she was blonde and buxom as Charlotte, it was all the same to him. He used cruder words, and spoke in some bastard Serbo-Croat, but I caught the gist. I slipped one of Crowe's gold coins to the hostess, and whispered that there'd be another if he left too many visible marks on the girl. She took that coolly, and said there'd be another whatever happened, and would we like to proceed downstairs? She shoved Konstantin in the back, and he cheerfully let himself be led towards the wide staircase in the corner of the room, up and down which trailed jaded jades, and their eager or sated charges.

"Up to Heaven, or down to Hell, *n'est-ce pas*, Devlin?" twittered No-Count Cagliostro.

"Shut your gob, you oul' *poupée*, " I spat at him. It's not his morals I object to, mind, but the airs and graces. The Devil knows, I'm no one to give lessons and 'thou shalts' and 'shalt nots', but this villain made my stomach turn. At least, he did now. We'd had some rare old times in the past, but Cagliostro had begun to give out rumours of his own gifts, in the esoteric arts, and to disparage mine. And we couldn't have that, especially when he was nothing but a two-

sous Satanic, who loved the titillation of sacrilege, and the thrill of committing Inverted Sin with choirboys that only the most devout of Catholics can feel. I cannot respect one who believes in sinning only for the twisted pleasure he gets from his own remorse. He made to stand, making sure one of his imps was there to hold him back.

It was then that she appeared. The comic turn of the little *travestis* was over, and they were bowing to much applause and laughter, and for their encore kissed again most sweetly. They skipped off the stage, and were engulfed with admirers, who vied to offer them tributes, Champagne, money, no doubt. But then there was a mournful wheeze of an accordion, and the lights seemed to dim, and the din to fade. Thomas and I both looked towards the stage, where a little waif slipped between the high red velvet curtains, to the limelight. Her hair was dark as ravens, hanging halfway down her back, her eyes as black as midnight, and her skin brown as berries. Her loose, flimsy, once-white blouse hung off one shoulder, and she wore a plain black skirt, tattered at the ends, showing her bedraggled petticoat, and bare feet beneath. A red scarf was knotted round her waist, and a golden bangle at her wrist. Charlotte returned, and asked would she show us to our berth below, but I shushed her, and said we'd wait; the Gyspsy Girl began to sing.

If you have heard the lonely songs of *sean nós* quavered by an old woman beside a turf fire in the hills around the Black Valley, or if you have heard the forlorn husky lament of a *fado* singer bring herself and the house to tears, in the Bairro Alto of Lisbon, then you will understand, that hush that fell upon the hilarity and ribaldry of the room. The accordion's opening faded, and her voice took over, slightly cracked, slightly coarse, but rich, and full of longing. The melody took strange turns and liquidly ran over grace-notes that set the ear on edge, then half-resolved, then shifted once again. It sounded like a thing one might hear sung among the Kabyle of the Atlas Mountains, or the lament of a woman as a ship pulled away forever from the dock, in Galicia, or on the Isle of Skye. It sang of loss, and the wind in the mountains, and death by water. It told of the heartache that no love could soothe, of the solitude no wine could wash away. She closed her eyes as she sang, and one hand came up in a gesture of a touch ungiven, and then tangled in a handful of her hair. I sneaked a glance at Thomas. He looked haunted.

PART IV

The song came to an end, a tearful, tearing, dying choke. She hung her head.
There was no applause. I saw some of the merrymakers shift uncomfortably,
and then quick as that, the accordion began a whirling waltzing tune, and she
whipped up her head, and clapped her hands above, and pulled from nowhere
a little set of chimes she shook between her fingers. Now she sang more lustily;
though still an eerie, gloomy tune, it was a livelier one. This one I understood, for
it was in Italian, and I knew that Thomas would too. Of course, I knew it anyway,
for I taught it to her, though she had to put the Italian on it herself, as mine's
not up to composition. Shouts and whistles joined her this time, and she tossed

her tousled hair, and whisked her skirts, then leapt at one point onto the nearest table, scattering bottles in her sinuous dance. This time she addressed her song, as she wandered through the room, now to this man, now to that, now to a young lady who sat smoking primly at a table full of pale young *poètes symbolistes*. I sang along softly, with the original words. She spotted me as she came to the final verse, and began to make her way towards us, her little white teeth flashing in her fierce smile. Ah, Demetra! I sighed, and held my heart.

As the song reached its end, suddenly there was a whine of a fiddle, playing along, coming from the upper gallery, that ran around the top of the high room. Lost in the smoke and dim light up there, one could not make out who played. Demetra's voice faded on the last line, and she looked around, above, her dark brows furrowed. The fiddle took up the tune, and played a merry variation, made it jaunty, in a mocking, sing-song way. Old Tortoise-Head, who did his duty on the accordion as well as piano, gamely kept the tune going, even picking up the pace a little. Demetra walked quickly over to us.

"Ah , Signor Devlin!" she greeted me chirply enough, but I could see she was slightly disconcerted. "*Allora! Salire o scendere*? You going up, or you go down?"

"What do you say then, Thomas, would you follow this one to the Underworld? I wouldn't trust her myself ..."

"What does it mean?" he asked, bewildered, but slurred and blurry-looking now, "What's all this up or down everyone keeps on about?"

"All will be clear. Come with me, Signor Tomasso. We will go down together."

She took him by the arm, and winked at me, then led him towards the dim-lit doorway beneath the balcony. I went to follow, and saw, coming down the wide staircase on the other side of the crowded room, an enormous swarthy man in a long, tattered coat, with a fiddle braced beneath his chin, his huge hands wielding the bow and dancing along the strings furiously, the instrument tiny as a child's toy in those great paws. He wore a broad-brimmed hat pushed low over his face, and stalked down the stairs like a great jungle cat, fiddling all the while. It seemed I knew him from somewhere; it seemed his gleaming eye roved across

PART IV

the crowd in search of someone. I turned, and saw Demetra disappear through the doorway, and down the narrow stair. Once more unto the breach, I said to myself, and followed, pushing through the raucous throng.

[Most irritatingly, Devlin's account ends here, leaving out the remainder of the night's events. I could fill them in myself from memory, but that would be but my account of what I could recall from what was told, in turn, to me. I leave this ending as it is, knowing that the next document to which we turn fills in some of the sequel in a most unexpected manner. I am not proud of it, but Devlin's feckless ability to abandon a task in mid-course has still, at this distance of years, the power to annoy me intensely. I have no doubt that this would please him. – W. Crowe]

PART V

Thomas MacGilpatrick's Paris Journal – November 1894

Woke very late again. I seem to remember knocking, and Damien's calling for me to get up, and asking was I well, but I hadn't the strength to respond, or to untangle his summons from the nets of my devious dreams. I have not been right since the night walking the streets with Devlin. It seems distant now, and all disjointed. I woke the next day only at sunset, with a feverish, oppressive gloom on me. They sent to wonder where I was, as I had missed all my meals and the service for All Saints' Day, and I gave out I was ill. Late that night Brother Pierre looked in on me. I could not meet his eyes.

I do remember this: seeming to come to, walking behind Devlin, toiling uphill, walking forever through a pale misty dawn light. We must have been coming up the Montagne Sainte-Geneviève. There was the Panthéon, looming beside us. Finally we came to the gates of the College. I looked around, and could hardly see straight, nor stand straight. Devlin banged on the door with his stick, and the Gatekeeper opened, eventually, clanking his keys. All of this passes before my mind's eye in silence, senseless.

Brother Pierre appeared at the door, and Devlin said some words, and the Brother Gatekeeper... he flung something. No. He swung his arm over his head, in his hand was a star of darkly shining metal, it seemed; it hung frozen in the air, and Devlin cowered. He brought it down upon Devlin's head, knocked off his hat, swung again, and Devlin roared and cursed, and Brother Pierre swung the metal star again, and it struck Devlin across the face, and Pierre seemed to cry "*Vade retro me, Satana!*" Devlin grasped up his hat and ran, shouting back what sounded like "*via brevis,* arse *longa, Frater Petrus*". The Brother put an arm around me, and I remember no more.

Tonight, he gave me to understand that he would say nothing to the Rector, but that I ought to look to my prayers, and look to my soul. Would that I could follow his advice. My mind is full of terrible fragments of that night, and a restlessness, and an awful guilt and foreboding. Damien said, last evening, that I only suffered what I deserved, in payment for my night-long debauch. I know he meant only drink – but I have had too much wine on other occasions, and I know what that feels like.

I feel a great weight of Sin on my conscience, and at the same time a great revulsion for the remedies that are to hand. Were I to seek the confessional, what could I say? Were my sins of Thought only, or of Word, or Deed? My memory is all disordered. We seemed to walk, that night, the streets of an Unreal City, peopled with phantoms. Devlin dances amid the fiery embers that remain, like a Genius of Mischief, and the goblin-guide that we acquired slinks in his shadow, the boy Konstantin. And behind all is the secretly smiling face of the Italian Girl, and the touch of feverish skin. What have I done?

Fractured images and snatches of words and songs, strange flavours and perfumes ... My mind is consumed with hopeless rage and shame, and my body revolts. I am perpetually thirsty, but cannot stomach solid food. These words begin to dance before my aching eyes as I write ...

Monday, 5th November

Little better. Walked a while in the afternoon in the Luxembourg Garden. The faces of the people passing oppressed me with their ugliness, their banality. How could so many each be the seat of a human consciousness, and devote it to the sating of their sordid lusts and appetites?

While I walked, I felt a dark stirring in the corners of my vision, as if something followed just behind, as if some malignant Shadow dogged my heels. I quickly returned here.

PART V

Tuesday, 6th November

The doctor they have brought to see me is none other than "Doctor Crowe". I was somehow not so surprised. He is well-known here, Br. Manus tells me, as a very devout and knowledgeable man of Science. He sat at my bedside for a long while, asked me many questions concerning the events of Hallow Eve. He asked me did I ever celebrate it at home in Cork, did I call it Oíche Shamhna, the old way. I told him we only had games and stories with Mama, like anyone, when we were children. He made me tell him all I remembered of what I'd done and where I'd been with Devlin. He said I would soon be well again, but must be careful, and must foreswear such riots, especially in Devlin's company. He gave me a draught to drink, and advised me to attend to my prayers. I have tried; the words are as ashes in my mouth. I seem to be suspended between half-sleeping and half-waking, and my dreams are vivid and violent and fleeting, leaving only a desperate unease, in my mind and in my body.

Wednesday, 7th November

Brother Pierre came to see me this morning. He sat and said nothing a long time, just looked. I lay still on the bed. Could not look at him. His breathing heavy, smelling of wine. He put something in my hand, and left. A small Rosary, only one string of beads – a single Decade – at one end a ring, at the other a flattened crucifix, of some dull metal. There are small symbols stamped around the Christ figure: a Cup for the Last Supper, the Spear that pierced His side, three Nails, the Hammer that drove them, a Halo of Thorns. Seen one of these before. From during the Penal Times in Ireland, to be hidden down sleeve in case caught by English. Ring goes on each finger, then thumb, for counting Decades. My lips would not form the words. My mind recoils from prayer. I hold it tighter as I write. The weight, the edges. I become calmer.

Crowe stayed for longer today. Since he gave me the sleeping-draught I do sleep easier and sounder, and am less troubled by strange dreams. He is a reassuring presence. A man in his middle-thirties, I would say, though looking sometimes younger, sometimes much older. He is clean-shaven, like a priest, and has dark hair cut short. Indeed, there is an air of the priest about him, and something of the sadness and resignation of one who has measured himself against that calling and found himself – or been found – wanting.

He *is* a Doctor of Medicine, but a Doctor of Philosophy and Theology as well, he seems to hint. I do not ask him many questions; his melancholy air of mystery forbids it, and it is mostly he who questions me. He asks me about my youth, about my family, about books I've read, and thinkers I have studied, about my education at the College and then the Seminary, and my time in Rome.

Unlike Devlin, whose talk ranged all over, who seemed to converse for the pure pleasure of encountering another enquiring mind, Crowe seems to submit me to some strange Catechism of his own devising: he questions me on minutiae of doctrine, on the nature of the Holy Spirit, on the questing thought of the Scholastics, on my knowledge of the *impasses* in which the great Heresiarchs lost themselves. Each time, he follows a line of questioning, nodding and pausing after each response, until something – something I say, or some other thing? – brings him to a stop, at which he brightens, and speaks of things of no consequence for a short time, then withdraws.

I cannot speak to his motives or his purpose, but his subtle questions seem to calm me, and I often pursue my reading for an hour or two after he leaves. I feel I may be strong enough to return to my studies very soon. Crowe's gentle drawing out of my faculties has left me much refreshed, and eager to follow up some of the ideas he has sparked off in my mind. He offers to bring me any books I need, or indeed to give me access to his library, as soon as I feel strong enough. For the present, I restrict my exercise to short walks in the courtyard. My meals are brought to me by Br. Manus, and I need see no-one, indeed feel very little inclined for any company but that of Dr. Crowe.

PART V

Yesterday was brighter than the rain and mist of the last week, and I went to walk in the Luxembourg, feeling refreshed after a night of dreamless sleep. As soon as I entered the gates of the park, I was caught by the arm in a strong grip. It was Konstantin. The daylight does nothing to improve his degenerate physiognomy. I tried to shake him off, but he scampered along by my side.

He said the Gentleman (by which I took him to mean Devlin) had told him to keep an eye on me, and to look after me when I went abroad, particularly at night. I told him in no uncertain terms that there'd be no more night-time escapades for me. He made a dismissive sign, and said that was not the best thing, he had a message for me, but that carrying messages was thirsty work. I told him I wanted no messages from Devlin. He said it was not from Devlin, but from the girl, who he calls the *Romani*, with a sneer. Was she quite well, I asked, for I had a sudden sense of her having been in danger, the fear of pursuit, fear for her safety. The creature told me she was in tip-top form, and back to spreading her legs for a few *sous*. I went to hit him, and he danced out of the way, shouting that he wouldn't even lower himself to dipping his wick there for free. I was furious, God help me, and I went for him, but before I knew it, he had me pinned against a tree with his forearm jammed across my throat, choking me. If that was my attitude, he'd be off without delivering his message. His other hand was on the hilt of his sword under his coat, and he poked my ribs with it, hard. I held up my hands, and he let me go, sinking to my knees, coughing and in pain. He spat on the ground, and said the Gentleman sent his regards, and would see me soon, and he'd tell me that for free. Before leaving, he swore again at me, and told me that he'd have his eye on me, and though no-one else would trouble me, he might be tempted to give me a real beating, if I didn't mind my manners.

I staggered back to the College, full of rage at my weakness, both of body – to be beaten by a boy – and of mind, for I could not keep my thoughts from her.

Demetra. There. I write her name.

The dreams return, and I dare not increase the dose of the draught Crowe gave me any further. Already, the little flask is near empty. When he came to me today, I was not dressed, but sitting up in bed, and trying to turn my mind away from the dark avenues where it had wandered in the night. I wished for fresh air, and to walk in green places, but the rain hissed down unceasingly outside my window, in the narrow streets, upon the drab gardens behind the high, blind houses. The day barely seemed to dawn.

Crowe asked me to speak of these dreams. My mind recoiled from some of them, but I did try to express one repeated impression that remains often on waking. I seem to see vast polar Antipodean lands, places of night-voyages by ships, upside-down compasses and charts, and impenetrable, unintelligible interior empires. I can almost see those ancient maps of *Terrae Incognitae* on waking, and I seem to know what it is to walk the decks of great iron ships that churn the ice-floes, in perpetual night; muted flares of lanterns only make the darkness visible, and on a bleak headland as we pass, a Cyclopean Pharos burns with a cold blue flame against the starless sky[1].

Monday evening

Again, I dream of Her. Her eyes that burn like coals amid the fumes of a dark chamber, the heat of her body near mine. She brings a chalice to my lips. The smell of her is of musk and cinnamon, and she seems to kneel beside a couch upon which I lie, prostrate. She murmurs the responses to a chanted litany that drones in many voices within the vaulted chamber. Her hands touch me. We both drink from the cup. The smoky vapour all around us, strong incense, herbs flung on burning braziers. Ah! Am I dreaming or remembering?

Tuesday, 13th November

---

1 Still nothing from Mr Oates. No response for notes to last 10 pages. Bizarrely, I have started to have this same dream. I obviously need to get out more.

PART V

Crowe asked me today of the progress of my Novitiate. I told him I would be going on Retreat when I returned to Ireland, and would prepare then to pronounce my First Vows, would take to the cassock; my voice faltered as I spoke. The fact of my desisting from the Holy Offices, from receiving the Blessed Sacrament, the fact of my not having been to Confession... he knows as well as I that I am not fulfilling my obligations now. Br. Manus begins to hint that I should go to speak to the Rector. I cannot face the thought of that good, quiet man, sitting behind his desk under the high window, listening to me voice my anguish.

Crowe sighed at my words, and at what I clearly did not say. He seems to understand. I wonder if he has once been in my position, or has known the torment of evil dreams. His face, when I looked again, in the dim room, seemed drawn with the knowledge of Sin, with the pain of one who has known the Darkness.

Wenesday, 14th November

Father, why hast Thou forsaken me? I cannot write, and yet I must. The effort this requires... my head is pounding. Crowe has been. He refuses me more medicine, he says we must try another path. I must attempt to write these dreams. Last night. Last night I seemed to pass through Hell. No. That is too simple. Last night I dreamed.

I fretted at the fall of darkness, on a day already dark. I wished for sleep, for oblivion. I swallowed all that remained of the sleeping-draught, against Doctor Crowe's advice. As I tried to close the casement against the seeping fog, I saw a brazen moon riding rushing shreds of cloud rise above the roof-tops. It seemed a corrupted Host, a staring eye. The mist that pooled beneath the trees in the gardens below gleamed with unearthly light. I fell on my bed, half in a swoon, and I seemed to lay immobile as the window, not quite shut, let pour in the wan rays of spectral light, and curls of chill vapour seemed to coil through the aperture, invading the room. I lay thus paralysed for hours, so I thought, and all the while the damp cold crept around my limbs.

Then I seemed to hear the words of a song, echoing and faint, mournful.

It was Her song from that night, the grim, merry song. *No cantar' d'amor, svegli mia madre, lei dorme qui, accanto a me*[2]. But just its echo, solitary and thin. It faded. I rose, entranced, and went to the window. The full moon was high, a misty halo thrown by its spectral illumination. In the rolling silver vapour of the gardens, I saw two figures standing beneath a bare dark tree. Strange shadows played about them, and they were at first indistinct, but I leaned through the casement, and I reached out one hand to them, as if to touch them. The song returned, piping, shivering. *Nella mano destra, pugnal' d'argento, lei dice che non si può sposare...*The mist swirled, and I saw it was Demetra, in a thin white gown, and beside her, behind her, the tall Stranger in his long dark coat, his hat hiding his face. One hand held her by the shoulder, and the other came up slowly, holding to her throat a long wicked blade that flashed in the moonlight. She raised her arms, in salute or supplication. I fell back upon the bed.

I woke again, and now a candle burned in my room, and I was undressed, and lying warm in bed. A shadow passed before the candle. A soft voice murmured to me. I raised my head, half-opening my eyes. She stood at the window, fastening it against the night. Turning, she put off the hood of her dark cloak, and smiled. I asked her how she came there. Through the window, of course, she told me. She let her cloak drop from her shoulders as she walked around the bed. Come, she said, do not be afraid. Only put your hand upon my heart, and you shall not fall. She approached me, and took my hand, and laid it on her breast. Under her thin gown, I could feel the warmth of her skin, and the beating of her heart. She kissed my lips, and the light went out, and she was there, against me, and all was blind sweetness, and scent, and caresses, and tender struggle. I woke again from velvet darkness, and saw her for a moment crouched upon the window sill. She put her finger to her smiling lips, and was gone. I rushed to the open window, and saw only blackness, and the freezing gloom on which no moon shone. Once more, I slept. And seemed to wake, again.

The Shadow crept upon the threshold of my room, it whispered crawling words and insidious promises. I could not move. The door stood open, and the Thing came closer, spidery limbs stretching forth across the floor. It spoke words that hissed and whirred and prickled on my skin. I tried to reach for a

---

[2] An Italian translation of the American folk song, 'Silver Dagger', of possible Scottish origins. I heard a busker singing it on the way home this evening. Strange coincidence. Bet Oates would say it 'means something'.

PART V

light, but there was no candle by my bedside. Its cold fingers reached for me, its cold breath filled the room. I was frozen in terror and I tasted the dank odour of the grave all around me. Shadows rushed to my side, and beating wings seemed everywhere. I could not breathe.

Thursday, 15th November

Crowe has come again. I told him of my night-long vigil, unable to face the visions that would return when I close my eyes. I stayed up until dawn, pacing my room, writing the account of last night's terrible memories, burning down three candles. He says there is a way to fight this, but that I must trust him. I am to come to his rooms tomorrow, trying meanwhile to rest as much as possible. I do not want to rest. I cannot. I feel like going out, to walk the streets, to keep awake, to stay conscious at all costs. But what might not be waiting for me, in the shadows of a doorway, around the next corner? The night is full of terrors, if I leave this place. Even here, if I allow my eyes to close, what minions of Man's eternal Adversary will assail me? If I lay me down to sleep, what dreams may come?

[At this point, I break off from Thomas MacGilpatrick's Journal, which I found among the papers in his room, to go back on some of the same events narrated therein from another perspective: my own. After the 15th of November, the entries become increasingly erratic, and many are without date. The progress of the experiment thus far will be better understood when compared with my own notes, which I humbly provide as the next instalment. – W. Crowe]

PART VI

William Crowe's Record of Proceedings in the Matter of

Thomas MacGilpatrick

3ʳᵈ Nov. 1894

I had not thought that he would go so far. Devlin has been most rash, and has forced my hand. I had envisaged the Game as playing out over a period of months, not weeks – or days! – but he thrown all his resources at this opening gambit. The boy has been subjected to a veritable baptism of fire. Nevertheless, I believe that this may work to my advantage. I mean to gain access to him, as he recovers, and turn the effects of Devlin's Night of Mischief to my own account, and proceed with more cautious efforts.

Devlin has been with me, and submitted to me his "Account of the Long Night", as he calls it. I protested that it was not finished, and he laughed, and said he became bored with writing, and must go off on some frivolous spree. I despair of him. No doubt, from what he tells me, his own memory is clouded enough *vis à vis* the last few hours of their adventure; rather than keep a cool head, he decided to indulge himself, in the Opium Den beneath the Cabaret de la Sirène. If the facts from this point are blurred, so be it. I shall perhaps have the opportunity to reconstruct them myself at a future moment.

After much negotiation and discussion, we established upon the Board, the current state of play. Devlin has been improvident. He plays his Trumps as if the Game is to be won or lost on the first round. I must admit, however, that some few of his tactics have a certain breathless flair. We have chosen, then, to represent the events of the first turn thus :

Knight of Wands (Devlin), Knight of Cups (Thomas) pass via Sphere of the Moon, circumventing Silver Maiden (Sophia, already in play). Proceed by Path of the Fool (Devlin's first Trump, Trickster), to the Labyrinth (my hidden library, Devlin maintains! His audacity, to claim *my* place as a Sphere on *his* Path!). Devlin plays The Wheel of Fortune, thus ruling the night's events by Hazard. Crossing the Board: enter the Sphere of Romance. D. claims Spanish *frère lampier*, Fra Hiedra, as King of Wands. I concede the card (Hiedra – *lierre* – Laoghaire...very clever). D. claims Konstantin Belovuc as Knight of Swords. This seems appropriate. I concede the card. Romance and Adventure (the funeral *cortège* of the Knights of Santiago, the pursuit by the Night-Guard, *et caetera*) give way to the Devil's Path (D.'s third Trump, Siren). Move to the Crucible, Sphere of the Dying God. Princess of Pentacles put in play (Demetra). Devlin plays *my* card, Temperance, reversed, as Queen Mab, the Intoxicating One. I must concede the play. This constitutes his fourth Trump. There is some discussion regarding the Stranger, the tall Gypsy Fiddler who seemed to enter the Game at the Cabaret de la Sirène. He maintains that this is my playing the Death Trump. I tell him no, I know nothing of this man, and conserve the card in my hand. We adjourn.

I believe that it was too soon to attempt the Crucible, and that Thomas had not been adequately prepared. Of course, this reflects the fundamental difference between Devlin and myself, in matters of Illumination. His is the Path of Ecstasy, of Poetry, of Inspiration, Intoxication, and Derangement of all the Senses. Chaos, in other words. His Road of Excess, he believes, will lead somehow to the Palace of Wisdom. I, on the other hand, favour the more ascetic approach; through Rigour, Discipline, Meditation, and Initiation, one may attain *gnosis*, finally. There are Eternal Laws that must be respected, Hierarchies, Rituals. Then Ascension, Awakening, may be achieved. I had thought that Thomas, with his highly regimented, subtle Jesuit training would be far more ripe for my own approach. But there is, obviously, much of the Wild Celt in him still, as there is in Devlin. Furthermore, he is young, and has not tasted much of life. It is difficult to renounce what you do not know, as I can attest myself. Devlin's wild foray into the City of Dreadful Night seems unwise, but he has planted many seeds in the young man's mind, and it will be difficult to win him back to a more measured, more spiritual Quest. However, Devlin seems to have reckoned without the effect on the poor child's constitution; not everyone can emerge from a night of such decadence unscathed.

After Devlin had left, I considered for some time, then moved Thomas's piece from the Crucible back to the Sphere of the Moon, where I placed with him the King of Pentacles: Brother Pierre, the Keeper of the Keys, who shall guard him from Devlin's influence.

Me to play.

6th Nov. 1894

My message to Brother Manus successful. They sent for me to consult in this "Strange Case of Thomas MacGilpatrick, Novice S.J." Sat with the boy some two hours. He is most shaken. No coherent memories of night of 31st Oct. – 1st Nov. after 1.30 am, approx. Does not remember clearly smoking opium in vaults below Cabaret de la Sirène.

By my estimation, Thos had ingested at that point: 6-8 *oz* Absinthe (3 measures), 2 cups wine (with meal in house of Ben Hakim), 1/3 bottle (6-7 *oz*) of suspect *eau de vie* (possible impurities, certainly above 110° proof), 1 (or 2?) *hashish*-infused cigarettes (unused to effects of tobacco alone), unclear quantity of beer (highly watered, effect barely perceptible).

Details of ingestion of opium unclear (Devlin has not a scientist bone in his body!). Level of intoxication clearly sufficient for high degree of suggestibility. Combined with frankly melodramatic stimuli of improbable events to his imagination, plus sexual arousal provoked by Demetra's behaviour, her Image becomes powerful nexus of spiritual conflict/excitation/nascent obsession. Well played, I must admit.

Provide Thos with "sleeping draught" – Laudanum containing powerful Tincture of Opium, to prolong visionary/somniferous effects; also extract of *Hyssopus cuspidatus* and *Melissa officinalis* for calming, anti-insomniac effects, and suspension of *Atropa belladonna*. Initial relief from troubling dreams will give way to hypersomnia, increasingly intricate, hallucinatory visions, growing dependence on the opium. Increase admixture of Belladonna gradually, decrease "calming" agents. Monitor level of mental discomfort. Vulnerability, need for relief, is desired issue, rather than derangement. Must proceed with caution.

PART VI

Devlin complains of my use of the Brother Gatekeeper to limit his access. I maintain this is "fair play", considering his seizure of long turn involving several moves on Hallow Eve. His influence is neutralized, for the time being. We agree that my "treatment" shall count as my re-appropriation of the Temperance Trump, played right-side-up, in its aspect of Potion Preparation. I have prepared a horoscope for Thomas, having gleaned details of the date and location of his birth. He is born under Pisces, with Gemini rising (this explains his apparent dual nature), and the Moon in Scorpio. Things become clearer. I now play the Hanged Man Trump, to signify his Ordeal (Christic imagery well-enrooted in him fully justifies this). His piece is thus returned from the Crucible, through the Sphere of Romance, to the Sphere of the Moon. I turn the Moon Trump also, played reversed. Nightmare, leading possibly to the Moon Triumphant, or Initiation. Silver Maiden figure is blocked by Gypsy Girl piece. Must attempt to put her back in play.

9ᵗʰ Nov. 1894

My Catechism of the subject begins. Lines of questioning are prepared, laying groundwork for Dark Night of the Soul. He appears at times to have an inkling of what is occurring, as his answers become increasingly heterodox. His knowledge of Early Christian Heresy is quite impressive. This augurs well, for the Church, in teaching him what he is being trained to combat, has also implanted in him fascination for these dangerous ideas. I attempt to lead him towards certain mystical notions, and he follows, but at the last moment falls back on a still-strong Faith. Despite his doubts, it must be admitted that he has a true tropism toward sanctity. I see that he keeps about him at all times a curious single-decade rosary. Where does this come from?

He has left the confines of the College. Devlin has thus been able to put his Knight of Swords back in play, as Messenger. The effect on Thos has been to return Demetra to his obsessional thoughts. I had thought to lead him away from her, as an Incarnation of Sin, and bring him on the Path to Illumination thus. I must reconsider. His dreams had begun to show progress. The Dream of the Inverted World allowed me to steal the World Trump from Devlin, and return to the Sphere of Romance, but this time as Spiritual Quest. Then I proceeded to call into question all his beliefs, to shake the foundations of his vocation. Devlin agrees that the Vanquished Watchtower Trump is appropriate here. We proceed to the Realm of Secret Knowledge, and the Alchemical Great Work may begin. I shall reforge his shattered Soul in the image that I wish. I shall send Sophia to him, as an Angelic Vision. The Moon is full tomorrow night. I withdraw the supply of the potion. The effects of this withdrawal should include: insomnia, physical pain, acute melancholia, horrific nightmares. If, as I expect, he finishes what is left in the flask in order to sleep tomorrow night, all should go according to plan.

14th Nov. 1894

Curse Devlin! Curse his ingenuity! He has foiled my well-laid plans. In doing so, he has also subjected Thomas to a far more nightmarish experience than I had wished to provoke. I arrived at the Irish College, expecting to be let in by Brother Pierre. He was not in his lodge, it seemed. Neither did Sophia appear. Her presence had been blocked, as I now know, by Demetra. Eventually, I gained access, as a passing brother from the kitchens responded to my knocking. We found Brother Pierre in profound, swinish sleep, a flask of drugged brandy by his elbow. I believe Devlin used Demetra, or possibly Konstantin, to give this to the old Gatekeeper, knowing his weakness. I cursed myself for a fool. The atmospheric conditions were ideal, the Full Moon's light diffused through a cloak of creeping fog.

PART VI

When I reached Thomas's room, I saw the candlelight flickering below the door (locked), and heard unmistakable sounds from within. Demetra had achieved sexual congress with the boy. I stood there like an idiot until the sounds ceased within, and the light was extinguished. Poor child, I know the effect that this could not fail to have. If he had been possessed by the idea of the seductive Italian Gypsy Girl before, what heights of monomania might not be reached now! I waited, hidden round the corner of a corridor, until I was quite sure she had gone, and returned to find the door ajar. I had not meant to deploy such a trick, but there was no option.

I pulled from my bag a small censer, and lit in it that terrible Persian incense I went through so many trials to acquire. I pushed the censer across the threshold of the chamber, and waited. My own mouth, I covered with a scented cloth, against the hallucinogenic effects of the incense. When I was sure that he had breathed enough of this Stuff of Nightmares, I stood, my cloak about me, in the doorway, and began to whisper dark prayers, and insidious incantations. I saw him toss and turn upon the bed, and whispered of his Sin, and of his Damnation, of the Empty Promises of the Abyss. He moaned in pain and terror. I snuffed the incense, and withdrew. I wish I had not been forced to proceed thus, but Devlin's audacity must be countered by my own. Dark things are thus brought into play.

Devlin was waiting for me in my rooms when I returned. I received him coldly, and he laughed. When I told him what I had done, he was enraged. How dare I transform a thing of Beauty, the gift he gave the boy, into a thing of Nightmare? I bade him a firm goodnight. In the Stygian Realm of Lead and Lodestone, whence I had hoped to bring the poor child on the Path to Illumination, I reluctantly turned the Magus Trump, inverted. The Dark Magician leads him down that terrifying path, and returns him to the Crucible.

15ʰ Nov. 1894

I do not understand. In Thomas's confused account of his "dreams", delivered to me today, fruit of a long, wakeful night, there are elements that do not make sense. He was in no state to report his experience yesterday, being much distressed. I let him sleep, and urged him to write down what he had seen. Has residual effect of the large dose of my potion, combined with the incense, caused him to elaborate on what occurred? I do not know. His account of Demetra's succubus-visitation is coherent with my understanding of what she did, but the previous element, where he saw her below his window with the Stranger? Devlin claims this did not happen, and to have no knowledge of this other Figure. The girl is nowhere to be found. I must proceed to the employment of another technique, *id est*, the application of Hypnotism to the subject. I bid him prepare. Another sleepless night should render him intensely suggestible, through exhaustion and mental anguish. We shall see.

16ᵗʰ Nov. 1894

He arrived at my rooms looking haggard and sleepless. I brought him to the study, where I made him as comfortable as possible. Then I bade Sophia enter. He was much disturbed, initially, at her presence. When I explained the procedure I proposed, and justified her attendance as both witness and recorder of the experiment, he seemed to calm. She, as ever, was exemplary. Soothed the boy with some kind words, made herself generally agreeable and sympathetic. Her influence returns, quite naturally, and she appears as Opposite Image to Demetra, as intended. As I told him, her knowledge of the science of Hypnotism, of Medicine, and her ability to take short-hand notes of all that passed, were invaluable. She would also act, as I said, as witness and arbiter, in case my own highly-focused attention should neglect any danger to either him or to myself. With his agreement, we proceeded.

Here follows the manuscript of the session, prepared by Sophia Walker from her own notes taken at the time :

Hypnotic Trance Induced in Subject Thomas MacGilpatrick, Friday 16th November, 1894, by Master William Crowe, at residence of Same, 122 rue du Bac, Paris. Record established by Mrs Sophia Walker, present as Witness

71   PART VI

Subject in high state of anxiety, calmed by administration of decoction of Valerian and Verveine in tea form. Master Crowe begins Hypnosis, achieving tranquilizing effect with mantra-repetition of prayers. Subject holds small rosary-beads in left hand; joins in recitation of prayers after initial resistance. Four passes with Silver Pendant suffice to induce preliminary trance. Questioning of Subject begins.

Crowe – On the night of Hallow Eve last, you went abroad with Stephen Devlin... Do you know Stephen Devlin?

Subject – Yes.

Crowe – Do you remember passing over the bridge?

Subject – Yes.

Crowe – Do you remember eating a meal in the house of Dov ben Hakim?

Subject – Yes.

Crowe – You walked to Les Halles, passing by the Torre de Santiago (Subject continues to confirm), meeting a Lamp-lighter Monk named Hiedra...After a confrontation between this monk and members of the Royal Night-Guard, you escaped in the company of a boy named Konstantin Belovuc...You continued your journey Northward, along the Rue Saint-Dionysius, and came to the Cabaret de la Sirène...Do you remember?

Subject – Yes...there is...I see a darkness approaching.

Crowe – Let us move into that darkness. You encountered, in that place, an Italian girl named Demetra Neri (Subject confirms)...With her, you proceeded to the vaults below La Sirène. There, you partook of an intoxicant. What were the circumstances? Try to see the scene before you...Bring us there with you ...

Subject – The lights...very dim. Smoke everywhere. My eyes sting. She is there. She comes to me...in her hands the tray. Places it on the table beside my couch. Devlin is there. He... he smokes from a pipe. A woman holds it to a burning glass. He laughs. She is beside me. I drink...the smoke...I drink the smoke...There is singing...They are all around us...she lies with me on the couch...my hands in her hands...her hands on my face...my chest...hot... burning herbs upon the brazier...she licks the sweat from my brow...she brings the Chal-

ice...we drink together...cool, and then burning...I repeat with her: I have fasted, I have drunk the kykeon, I have taken from the kiste, and after working it have returned it to the kalathos...darkness...and ecstasy...I join the dance...they chant obscenities...Íakch', O Íakche!...the Ritual moves towards the End...Omphalos...Oneiros...Ourobouros... Devlin is crowned with the Laurel...Demetra is crowned with Ivy...the drumming...yes![1]

Responding to increasing agitation of the Subject, Master Crowe makes three new passes with the Pendant, returns Subject to deeper level of trance.

Crowe – Move forward in time...forget the Ritual...Let it leave your mind. Surround the Ritual in brilliant bars of blue light. It will remain there, until I ask you to access it again. What happens next? After you have left the Cabaret de la Sirène, who is with you?

Subject – We are sitting...we are rolling, moving forward...we are on a cart. Moving over cobblestones. Night air is cold, very cold. They are laughing. Konstantin is drunk. Devlin and Demetra are lying in the back of the cart, between the metal milk-barrels. They whisper to each other. I look at the street behind...(long pause)...There is something... something approaches...There is...it is the Stranger. He is following...Look! He is here!... In his left hand is the Silver Dagger, in his right he holds a Naked Flame...he comes!

Intense physical agitation on the part of the Subject. Crowe immediately returns him to deeper level of trance. We consult on whether it is advisable to continue. Crowe decides to attempt one more regression.

Crowe – Do not enter the moment of the Stranger's approach. Tell us only the result. Without revisiting this event, tell us where the pursuit ended. Provide salient details only; remain calm, remain detached from the events. Once this account is over, you will take these events, these images, and you will surround them also with brilliant bars of blue light; they will remain inaccessible to you, until I unlock them, in a future trance-state. Begin.

Subject – The Stranger pursued us. Devlin saw him, when I called out. He pushed two of the metal barrels from the cart into the Stranger's path. He kicked Konstantin, but the boy was sleeping soundly. Devlin pushed the driver of the cart off into the street. He took the reins and whipped up the team of horses until the cart gained much speed. Demetra threw something behind us, a kind of dust. It seemed to create a cloud. We...I choked on

---

[1] [NB look up that book on Eleusinian Mysteries. It was in Ancient History Reading Room at the Ecole Normale Supérieure]

PART VI

the dust.

(long pause)

Crowe – Where did you go then?

Subject – We ended at the Bridge of Arts. Day was beginning to break. Demetra sang her song again, very softly, just for me. She held my hand. Konstantin sat by the rail, complaining of a headache. Devlin played a little flute. It was very cold. He gave me a small clay pipe, to warm my hands at its bowl. He lit it for me...Then...I saw...I saw attached to the rail of the bridge, both sides, chains of silver, floating...at the end of each chain... over the river...on each chain, a little heart hangs...bleeding, burning hearts, hanging in the air, chained to the bridge...OH! (Subject exclaims very loudly, becomes agitated. Crowe persists)...He's there!

Crowe – Who is there, the Stranger?

Subject – Yes! He has found us! He speaks: He comes to take what is his...Demetra is his... he holds in his hand the Naked Flame, he bears the Silver Dagger...the Chains are his, and she is his, he says...He comes!...Rushing at us, his black cloak spreads like wings, but no! She is gone...Demetra has jumped the rail...I see her then, she has landed on a barge...It drifts off down the river, he cannot cross the running water...Konstantin jumps to meet him, he draws his sword...clashing of steel on silver...Devlin...Devlin takes my hand, we run...We run...we run...there...he will not follow now, it's her he wants...oh ...

Subject breathes heavily, panting, as if exhausted from physical exertion. Master Crowe makes a further set of passes with the Pendant, returns him to a deeper trance.

Subject is left to sleep. Master Crowe dismisses me, saying he has much to consider, and that he will supervise the transition of the Subject to natural sleep.

[Record ends]

PART VII

Thomas MacGilpatrick's Paris Notes – November-December 1894

Some days have passed quietly, since I last was with Doctor Crowe and Sophia – she says I must call her Sophia – and the incidents of the past weeks seemed to fade, to recede in my mind. There was within me a strange, hollow peace, a newfound lightness. It was, in one way, not unlike the clean whiteness of the Soul one feels after making a good Confession, and after receiving once more the Blessed Sacrament. A fresh start, so to speak. By the operation of his Hypnotical experiment, Doctor Crowe had been able to "pluck from the memory a rooted sorrow, raze out the written troubles of the brain, " and I no longer needed to unburden myself of Sin, for there was no Sin, there was only knowing, and not-knowing.

I went to Mass in the Chapel yesterday, and my mouth moved with the responses, and I took the Eucharist, but all the while I knew that these were only external signs, and that there was, somewhere, a deeper, more powerful Truth, from which the Veil had been pulled aside for a short time, and now fell back in place. Crowe had said some things, had intimated that there were ways of transcending this poor shimmering surface that we know as the World, to a brighter, far more terrible World Beyond. But he told me to return to my studies, to return to the path of my Novitiate, to forget all that had passed. I cannot.

Then yesterday afternoon, I saw Her again. I walked across the park, my mind strangely empty, breathing the cool, clear air, and the scent of Autumn bonfires, seeing the leaves a riot of scarlet, amber, gold – a pyre of the year. A voice called to me, and I thought for a moment it must be Sophia, but no, this was a stranger. She ran to meet me, laughing, breathless as she caught up to me, and took my arm with the affection of an old friend.

She wore plain, dark clothes, a black straw hat, with two tattered poppies of red silk in the brim. Around her shoulders, she had a moth-eaten fox fur, and her gloves were old and worn. Her hair was pinned up beneath her hat, but some strands escaped, curled black against her olive skin. Demetra. Was this paltry creature the Seductress that had haunted my dreams? In her brave Sunday best, in her vulgarity, and her poverty, she was devoid of all threat, of all attraction. She spoke to me in Italian, for she knew I'd understand, and chattered gaily of this and that. She had heard of my illness from Devlin, and said she lit a candle for me in Saint-Merri every time she passed. Was I quite recovered now? She had wished to see me again, and to have the chance to speak to me.

I answered her coolly, and said it was perhaps not fitting for a man in my situation to be seen with a woman in hers. I wished her well, of course, and hoped that she might find her way back to the Fold, from where she'd strayed. I trusted there were Charitable Organisations that might help one in her case, but for myself, I regretted that there was nothing I could do. Bidding her good day, I turned to leave. Her black eyes seemed to fill with tears, and she asked me had it all been nothing to me. I told her I could not imagine what she meant, and walked quickly on. I knew now where I was going: to speak with Doctor Crowe.

Friday, 23rd November

Of course, Master Crowe had been waiting for me. That first day, he agreed to begin my Preparation, to open to me the Hidden World, to set me on the Path. Sophia arrived not long after I did, and once he had told her she might speak freely before me now, I understood. She has been his student for some time. We would receive instruction together. He would report to my superiors that he was to tutor me in philosophy. He said to me that everything, before, had been preparing me for this.

There are those who go through the Dark Night of the Soul, and fall back on simple faith. And there are those for whom nothing can ever be so simple, henceforth. Ordination to the Priesthood is one thing, he says, but every religion since the dawn-times has had also a Secret Inner Initiation, into the Mysteries

PART VII

known only to a few. For it is given, to some Chosen Ones among us, to no longer offer pleading prayers, as supplicants to an indifferent, uncaring God, but to command, by the force of Pure Will, the Powers of the World Above, and the World Below. Would I learn to craft my Soul, and reach perfection – Illumination – in this life, and not wait meekly for the life to come?

He read to us from the Gospel of Saint Thomas, which is not admitted to the Bible as most know it. He repeated the phrase, as he stood at the window: "I shall give you what no eye has seen, what no ear has heard and no hand has touched, and what has not come into the human heart." Sophia took my hand. She whispered: "You know this, you have always known this, always desired this, have been approaching this forever. We shall go together, you and I ..."

* * *

I will write no more here. This book is finished, and I will inscribe a new Name, in a new Book. I put away childish things. I saw only through a glass, darkly, then. Now, soon, face to face. She and I, it is to be soon. She told me: Simon Magus made only one error, and it was to try to buy power. The true price of power is nothing less than a Soul.

* * *

Something is wrong. She was not there today, nor yesterday, or the day before. Crowe says not to worry, but he is worried. The dreams are becoming more intense. He says this is natural, and that I should repeat the Exercises, and the First Banishing Ritual, to protect myself as I sleep, for I am most vulnerable now.

I seem to wake, many times, each night, and I must go to the window. The Stranger stands below, beneath the tree. Silently, he calls to me.

* * *

Where is she? We cannot proceed without her! I cannot go on... Crowe knows something, he will not tell me. He will not give me another flask of the sleeping-draught. I cannot sleep, I am never more than half-awake. In the streets, there is Something at all times, just beyond the range of my vision, that follows me.

* * *

Went to Devlin's studio...everything is gone, the canvases, the books, the furniture. All is as if abandoned many years ago. I need his help, I must reach him, how to reach him?

* * *

We are running out of time...

Dream of a pool in a forest glade. She is there, beneath the water, her loose hair flowing golden-green around her white limbs. She seems to sleep. She drifts down into Shadow. And there is Demetra, she smiles and puts her finger to her lips, and then her eyes widen in terror and she is pulled down down down.

PART VII

There is another, there. I cannot see her, but I know. Poor Milly, she is in the Pool, with the Lost Girls. Maybe they don't want to be found.

* * *

I will find her myself. If Devlin will not appear, if Crowe can do nothing, as it seems, I will go to Him. The Stranger waits beneath my window.

He waits only for me to give him a sign.

[I add here the short note that was found folded in his coat, scrawled in pencil, at the end. – W. Crowe]

One! There is only One! And what I have seen...Everything has been a Lie! He is there now, and I am ready. I go to pay her price.

PART VIII

Devlin's Parting Letter

Paris, 23rd December, 1894

Crowe,

I received your note. I will not be coming, and I trust I can leave you to take care of the necessary arrangements. By the time you read this, I will be gone. Paris is no place for me in Winter, and I go, like a swallow, to seek the South. I advise you not to dally there either. I am sure the climate in the city is become quite unhealthy, as you'll find.

Your accusations do you no credit. Did you think we merely played at chess? Did you think a wager with the stake of a Human Soul could be lightly made? If you had only let me still play my part, perhaps some of what occurred could have been averted. You set the boy in search of things of which he never should have known; you promised him too much, too soon. All I had wished to do was to open his eyes, and let him feel that ecstasy, and see those visions, that I have always known. I never said I'd give him Power.

You knew that the girl and I had had previous dealings, and that we had made some – I see it now – imprudent explorations, questionable vows. I never thought those promissory notes would be called in. I do regret the end that she came to, certainly. But she went into this with her eyes open. She was innocent of nothing. You say that she had tried to tell you? Why did you not listen then?

Forgive and forget, live and learn. Wash your hands of this, as I have done, my friend – as I remain yours, truly,

S. Devlin

81

PART VIII

PART IX

William Crowe's Testimony

It has ended. It should not have come to this. What began as an idle wager, for the amusement of two trifling gentlemen, has ended darkly indeed.

My plans had come to fruition. The boy came to me, and asked me to admit him to the Secret Path. Devlin had failed, in his last gambit. A Soul laid waste is not the place to seek kindness, or gentleness, or mercy. Thomas wished now to transcend that weak flesh which had betrayed him. With Sophia as his fellow student, he renounced his Novitiate in the Church of Rome, and came with us into that Hidden Temple. All was being prepared. He progressed remarkably quickly. Devlin attempted to distract me with talk of some Other Influence that was abroad, something that had come, attracted by the Mystery Play that we enacted, that sought to intervene, between us and our goal, and steal the Soul that we had promised to Enlighten. I paid him no mind, thinking he was telling tales, seeking attention, as is his wont.

I should have known that something was not right, when the girl began to speak of being followed. We had thought her capably guarded, by Abel Guest. I knew, of course, that she had made enemies, in England, among the Sect that her late husband had fallen into; they had wished to use her for their own ends, and her escape had been a great frustration to them. But I knew nothing of the Gypsy, the one who had appeared during that Long Night, the Stranger in the ragged coat. I thought it an invention, an opium vision. Devlin had the story from her, but had not given it the credence he should have. Her mother's people, as it turned out, had indeed promised her to Him, when she would be of age. All this is clear, now.

She disappeared on the 12th of December. We had fixed the 13th as the beginning of the Working that would Initiate her into the higher Order, considering the Feast of Saint Lucia to be a fitting one for this ceremony. Only now do I understand why she was so eager to proceed. She thought it might protect her. We searched, and found only the body of Abel Guest in her rooms near the Observatoire, his throat slashed through. Konstantin, we had ordered to watch Thomas, to follow him everywhere. At this point my young acolyte became increasingly erratic, and spoke of wild dreams and visions that were not those that the Path prescribes, or were distortions of them. I attempted to reassure him, but he would not listen. He had become terribly attached to Sophia, and refused to proceed without her, though I told him that it was perhaps advisable; in his incomplete stage of Metamorphosis, he was as helpless as the formless creature in the chrysalis, before the Imago is ready to emerge. At this point he escaped us, for a period of days. I do not know where he went in that time.

Finally, Konstantin brought him in, having scoured the streets for any trace of him. It was Hiedra, the Lamplighter, who had seen him, haunting the passages and alleyways near the Cabaret de la Sirène. He was filthy and starving, babbling about the Stranger, who it appears he had met. Now, too late, I began to take notice of this Other Influence. Indeed, my contacts around the city had alerted me, of the arrival of some foreign Power, whose very presence deranged all their Workings, their Invocations, their Scrying. I attempted to calm the boy, first through sedatives, and then through Hypnosis, but I could not bring him to a state of trance.

It was two days later, on the night of the 21st of December, that Devlin arrived at my door, and said he'd found her. She was in dire trouble, and she begged him to bring both me and Thomas to her. We followed Devlin through the shabby warren of streets just South of the Seine, and arrived at a grim-looking lodging house, where we were greeted by an old over-dressed woman who said "O, you are her three kinsmen from Ireland. She has been expecting you all day." She led us upstairs. Pale faces, haloed with untidy hair, peered at the doors, open a crack, along the gloomy landings.

When we entered the chamber, I was suddenly afraid. There was a ragged Sibyl by the bed, and a grimy lamp gave a faint light. The crone looked up, and shook her head sadly, and stood to leave. She and the landlady withdrew, and we approached the bed. I had not thought, I really had not thought. I had grown so used to seeing her as one thing, then the other, that to see her now in her natural state was a shock even to me. Thomas looked at her, and seemed to choke.

PART IX

There she lay, unconscious, the blankets pushed back from her in her fever, her thin nightgown soaked with sweat, her hair damp around her forehead. But there was no mistaking it. Her skin was neither pale as moonlight, like Sophia's, nor berry-brown, as Demetra's had been. Her hair was neither black nor silver-gold, but a fair, coppery colour. Wearing now neither disguise, with no subtle paint to change the shape and colour of her eyes, her mouth, she was only herself, and Thomas saw her as if for the first time. He fell to his knees. Who is this woman? he cried. Devlin and I could only look at one another. The boy grasped her hand in his, and tried to wake her. She stirred, moaned and murmured, and fell back into her unnatural sleep.

Then the light flickered and dimmed, and it seemed the windows rattled in their frames, as from a gale. A terrible chill pervaded the room, and the girl cried out in pain. Devlin became rigid, as I have seen him do before, and he began to speak Inspired words, that came from elsewhere, his voice hollow and booming:

"This woman has been the seat of all Follies, has been the Mistress of all Vice. She was promised to me, and gave herself to me. You three Foolish Men shall be as Witnesses. Do not come between me and my Heart's Desire. She is with child, and will give birth, to a thing Unseen, and it will be now. You shall abandon her, and you shall go from here, and you shall preach, as voices in the Wilderness, this terrible Annunciation ..."

Devlin fell in a faint, and the gale seemed to howl all around us. The girl upon the bed writhed, and arched her back, and let out a scream that froze my blood. Thomas rushed to the window, and threw it open, letting in a blast of dark air, and the sound of beating wings. "He is here, He has come!" he screamed. I fought my way to the side of the bed, and took the girl by the hand, in her agony. Bella, I whispered, Isabella, I am here, I am sorry, I am sorry, I did not know... Devlin, come to his senses, rushed also to her side. We held her hands, and spoke words and incantations, called on Powers and Guardians.

She whispered words now, calling something by many names: "Harsh Sweetness... Dear Bitterness... Beloved Darkness... O Solitude... O Little Loss..." The room was dark, but she glowed with an unearthly light, and suddenly, her struggles ceased, her eyes opened – neither ice-blue, nor black, but green, green eyes – and she murmured, "Thomas, sweet Thomas, please... You could have saved me, Thomas, please... If you had only loved me, Thomas, sweet Thomas... please..." And the light went from her eyes.

He had turned, at the sound of his name, from where he stood, rapt in awful fascination, looking out into the shrieking air. He came slowly to the bed, and his eyes were no longer wild. He knelt, with us, and took from his wrist that strange little rosary. He placed it in her hand, and kissed her forehead, and said: "Hush now. He will not have you. You are safe now. Here is love, at the last. I go now to pay your price."

He stood, and looked at us for a moment, whether with pity or with contempt, I do not know, then left the room. The flurry of wings, the dark howling of wind, the piercing chill, all faded, and the lamp flickered back to life. Isabella lay still, the beads clutched loosely in her unfeeling hand.

Thomas's body was found, many days later, beneath a certain tree, in the overgrown garden of an abandoned house, off behind the College. A young friend of his had happened to see it, from Thomas's window, as he looked there for a sign of where his friend had gone. The frost and snow had taken the body and turned it into a pale, inhuman, icy thing. Its eyes were wide open, and staring, and in its right hand, there was a long silver dagger, the blade encrusted with crystals of black blood, which beaded also at the ragged gash across his throat.

The authorities of the College left matters in my hands, and I arranged for his burial, unostentatiously, but honourably, in a plot that I own in Père Lachaise. The coroner, on my advice, recorded "Death by Misadventure", but I sorrowfully let fall enough hints in my correspondence with the family, that they did not ask too many questions, and allowed me to accomplish his interment with all possible haste. They have, at least, a grave to visit.

Bella Macrieff, on the other hand, was buried in an unmarked pauper's grave, in the Cimetière des Innocents. Devlin and I were the only mourners. The daughter of a wastrel Scottish father, descended from a Jacobite Laird who took refuge in Paris after the '45, and a music-hall artiste mother, of uncertain Italian

PART IX

heritage, with Gypsy connections, she lived a strange, short life. Educated in England and Switzerland, swiftly orphaned and disinherited, she had fallen in with artists and theatrical folk, working as a painters' model, and a cabaret singer, and then become involved with mystics, Rosicrucians, Diabolist Sorcerers... and with us. She was a very talented young woman, and played her last, dual role to perfection. Perhaps she could be said to have taken it too far. In all events – in all things – she knew what she was getting into.

AFTERWORD

As all correspondence from Mr Walter Oates at Savage House has ceased, I'm beginning to wonder whether this edition of *Unreal City* will ever see the light of day at all. I still haven't found my missing copy of the Olympia Press edition, *The Devil in a Woman's Form*. Is this all some kind of sick joke?

Meanwhile, the letters from whoever it is who signs himself "James Caulder" continue to arrive. Clearly, someone has done their research. Caulder's grandson, James, did disappear in Paris approximately ten years ago, and has not been heard from since. I tried to reach his mother, Angela, in Cork, but the phone number I have for her appears to have been disconnected.

Two nights ago, when I came back to my apartment, it looked like someone else had been there. My notes and files on *Unreal City* were scattered all over the room. Nothing else seemed to be missing. I took on this commission in good faith, but apparently, someone is trying to prevent this book from being published. I cannot imagine why this is.

I'm going to print this draft of the typescript and send it to Mr Oates at Savage House. When I tried to get a phone-number for the publishing house, Directory Inquiries informed me that no such business was registered in the Greater London Area.

This is beyond a joke, and I have better things to do with my time. Obviously, I will not be going to meet "James Caulder", as he requests. I hope whoever is behind this is very amused.

[handwritten note added below]

Apparently, Mr Mulholland has been the victim, or the perpetrator, of a convoluted literary hoax. Of course, none of the correspondence from "James Caulder" was found in the apartment. This manuscript, printed and bound with a white ribbon, was left on the desk. I don't think it will be any help to us in our inquiries as to the whereabouts of Tom Mulholland. There is no record in any Olympia Press bibliography of a novel called Unreal City or The Devil in a Woman's Form. I think this is a dead end.

Detective Inspector Peter MacIntyre,
Chief Investigating Officer.

Milton Keynes UK
Ingram Content Group UK Ltd.
UKHW051156111223
434150UK00011B/148

9 782494 927018